MEMORY AT BAY

CARAF Books

Caribbean and African Literature
Translated from French

Renée Larrier and Mildred Mortimer, Editors

MEMORY AT BAY

ÉVELYNE TROUILLOT

Translated by Paul Curtis Daw

Afterword by Jason Herbeck

[handwritten annotations:]
mom stands in for homeland.
grew up in french (martinique)
marmer past dies
— mom's childhood under dictator
— marie - Ann: present day
edile - childhood
- life as a first lady
edile takes care of marie ange

University of Virginia Press
Charlottesville and London

Originally published in French as *La mémoire aux abois*
© Éditions Hoëbeke, 2010

University of Virginia Press
Translation and afterword © 2015 by the Rector and Visitors
of the University of Virginia
All rights reserved
Printed in the United States of America on acid-free paper

First published 2015

9 8 7 6 5 4 3 2 1

LIBRARY OF CONGRESS CATALOGING-IN-PUBLICATION DATA
Trouillot, Évelyne, 1954–
 [La mémoire aux abois. English]
 Memory at bay / Évelyne Trouillot ; translated by Paul Curtis Daw ;
afterword by Jason Herbeck.
  pages cm — (CARAF Books: Caribbean and African Literature
translated from French)
 "Originally published in French as La mémoire aux abois © Editions
Hoëbeke, 2010"—Verso title page.
 Includes bibliographical references.
 ISBN 978-0-8139-3808-0 (cloth : alk. paper)—ISBN 978-0-8139-3809-7
(pbk. : alk. paper)—ISBN 978-0-8139-3810-3 (e-book)
 1. Duvalier, François, 1907–1971—Fiction. 2. Haiti—Fiction. I. Daw, Paul
Curtis, 1947– translator. II. Herbeck, Jason, 1971– writer of afterword.
III. Title.
 PQ2680.R656M4613 2015
 843'.914—dc23
                                                              2015000684

Cover art: Little Bird Collages: Stellar's Jay and *Hummingbird,* Diana Sudyka

CONTENTS

TRANSLATOR'S ACKNOWLEDGMENTS

My profound thanks to Évelyne Trouillot. It has been a rewarding privilege for me to engage with her powerful, compassionate novel. More than that, she graciously answered my many questions and provided indispensable guidance at every stage of this project.

I extend my deep appreciation to Jason Herbeck, not only for his insightful and enlightening afterword but also for his true collaboration and unstinting help whenever it was needed.

My sincere gratitude goes, as well, to everyone at CARAF/ the University of Virginia Press with whom I have worked. Cathie Brettschneider patiently steered me through the editorial process. The series editors, Renée Larrier and Mimi Mortimer, gave welcome advice and assistance, in addition to carefully reviewing the manuscript and perceptively commenting on it. The copyediting role was expertly discharged by Ellen Satrom, who spotted and rectified numerous lapses large and small. And the external readers deserve thanks for recognizing the novel's value and importance and for their very helpful remarks regarding the translation.

With much affection, I thank my wife, Carol, for her enthusiastic support and encouragement all along the way, and especially for her thoughtful comments on the manuscript.

Last, I would like to acknowledge the strong and resilient people of Haiti, so vividly and inspiringly brought to life by Évelyne Trouillot in all of her works.

For an explanation of words followed by an asterisk, please refer to the glossary.

MEMORY AT BAY

To Nady, Nadève, Shadine, and Ana Marie

To my longtime readers, faithful, enthusiastic, and demanding

To the memory of those children, men, and women
who died under the dictatorship; to the memory of those
who fought against it

To all women and men who believe that freedom
is worth fighting for

THE SURVIVOR AND THE MOTHER

speaking to my mother

I head home with the smell of the old woman's withered flesh on my fingers. The vision of her form sprawled limply on the bed like a nameless doll accompanies me through the streets of Paris. Why had they added that room to my list?

"Whatever you do, mademoiselle, don't reveal her name. No one should know who she is. Besides, we have no official confirmation. I thought you were only a child when you left your country. The dictator—I'm talking about the father, of course—was already dead when you were born, so you mustn't get carried away. Management has not authorized us to say that this woman is really his widow. In any case, this is no concern of yours."

Who does he take me for, that idiot of a director with his conspiratorial air? Even if I weren't the daughter of Marie-Carmelle, who suffered all her life from the horrors of the Doréval era, I would have recognized that woman's face. How could I forget it?

introduced as her mother's daughter

« »

Silence is ultimately the surest means of control. She realized this one morning at sunrise when the first sounds of the cleaning staff infiltrated the dreams of the patients still slumbering in the nursing home. The only solution lay in her ability to curtail all communication with the outside world. And so she withdrew into the silence of her thoughts, determined to resist the confusion that was threatening every shred of her ideas, intruding into her reminiscences and into the slightest empty space between word and image. She was content to delegate the tiresome everyday ministrations to the people paid to perform them. Like that well-built Algerian given the task of lifting obese patients who were too heavy for the young female aides. Or the African doctor who looked in once a week or not at all. Like that nurse of around sixty whose elegance reminded her of the good old days, when from beneath her fine silk petticoats she would gracefully reveal her Italian shoes. Or that dark-eyed young woman who often scowled furtively at her. And so, without regret she abandoned to them the responsibility of bathing, feeding, and caring for her.

It was their problem if they all took her to be more senile than she really was. They would stop trying to worm secrets out of her, stop regarding her as the strange beast of the facility. The one they point out to the relatives of the other patients. The one they mention in their phone calls as if by chance. The one around whom the mutterings linger long enough for the words "widow" and "dictator" to reach her. From now on, she would let them attend to her without a word. She would take refuge in her memory, but she would need a structure, a method, so that her thoughts would not tatter like the dingy sheets that covered her body.

« »

No doubt I should consider myself fortunate to have this lousy job. After all, I'm not a Frenchwoman by birth. What excellent luck to be able to wipe the wrinkled backsides of these old ladies that somebody has decided to put away in this nursing home, where life enters only on the sporadic occasions when an employee opens the door to breathe the outside air, smokes a cigarette near the window, or leans out over a sidewalk that taunts him to jump.

Yes, I do think about dying. I'm not a fighter the way you were, Maman. You who, despite your passport with its unloved colors, showed more determination and fighting spirit in your little finger than I'll ever have. Yet I was educated in the French Antilles, and I have a passport with the tricolored emblem of the French Republic. I can travel almost anywhere I like without a visa. I can certainly return to your island of a thousand problems and visit your grave without fearing in the pit of my stomach that I'll be refused entry on my return trip. But still, Maman, I can't stop thinking about nothingness, about the oblivion that could be mine, that lies so near and tempts me.

《 》

Above all, avoid dwelling on the colors of the sea, which she used to observe from the palace window while a luminous arc crowned the horizon in shades of orange and blue. She loved pausing there, if only for a moment, and it seemed to her at those times that she could catch the salty tang of the Caribbean. Wafting up to her above the old iron-roofed market with its intricate web of retailing and wretchedness, above the lower city with its streams of movement between the chaos of the avenues and the tranquility of obscure dead-end alleyways. Drifting over the stench of rancid sweat and foul water. Overpowering the moist scent of the freshly watered lawns and arriving at last to salute her. The sea, extending in the distance from north to south. Yet so near. Always at the limit of her vision. Always at the core of her memory.

《 》

I don't even have the option of refusing to care for this wizened old lady and taking the risk of being fired from this job: it's nothing special, but it allows me to survive with a semblance of dignity. Still, seeing and taking care of her keeps me awake at night. My nightmares have returned since you left. Latifa says she hears me moaning in the night and that my eyes look like two butterflies in a cage. I'm the perfect candidate for the advice she takes straight from her psychology textbooks. But my roommate doesn't grasp the scale of my distress. She thinks I'm just anxious about the monthly rental deadlines that roll around too quickly, in spite of all the yogurts and cheese sandwiches I eat in the guise of lunch and dinner. That I'm depressed because it seems less and less likely I'll ever have a little apartment all to myself, even one as cramped and dark as the one we share. Or because you left my life so abruptly, after taking up so much of it! All those reasons do enter in, especially the last one, but unfortunately things are more complicated than that.

In a pinch, if I went to a lot of trouble, I might find a job a little better suited to my qualifications, but why make the effort, and how would I go about it?

I know you owned several scraps of real estate in Quisqueya and that you would have liked me to go claim them. Seriously, Maman, can you see me turning up in your native city, Descailles, and wrangling with my cousins over a few scraggly plots of land and a tumbledown shack? You always overestimated my abilities, as if with my little degree in communications I could aspire to God knows what important position. You did so much with so little. But I'm not you, Maman.

Even if I've inherited some of your dreams in spite of myself.

All your stories of the dark years of the Dorévals come back and fill my mind. All those reminiscences poured out while you tucked me into bed at night, and as we made our way between home and school, from the kitchen to the bedroom, from Port-du-Roi to the French Antilles, and I from Martinique to continental France—"la Métropole," you called it. From the perspective of more than 150 years of Quisqueyan independence, you always pronounced that word with an indefinable blend of scorn, regret, envy, and resignation in your voice, bathed in anger and pride. Each emotion deeply embedded in its strongbox of memories, anecdotes, and appropriated incidents. Your country's tangled history came through to me in a tone that was at once aggressive, plaintive, and dignified. Like a desperate and beautiful murmur. In the image of your life.

« »

But for her own peace of mind, she has to return to that narrative. To reconstruct it, tell it to herself, without straying into sentimental or romantic digressions. And, most important, in an orderly way. Therefore, she will not begin with the Deceased. His was a presence so encompassing, so weighty, that she will save it for later. If time permits her to continue the voyage. In her own manner, without pressure or constraint of any kind. Like those cruise liners where the passengers are supposed to amuse themselves as they wish, eat as much as they want, and have a good time, even when the rolling of the ship makes them seasick, or suicidal impulses call out to them from the bottom of the sea. She would proceed at the pace of a distinguished woman, a Guardian of the Revolution, a first lady who does not hurry, though death intently awaits her. But she learned very early to keep a cool head at all times. At the end of her life, she would not dishonor herself before the image reflected in her mental mirror—the one we all consult when we look with closed eyes at our shriveled flesh. The Deceased would wait his turn. She would begin with her children, all four of them. Despite all the gossip, the rumors and conflicts, she never felt, never manifested, a preference for one or another. She loved them all. From the oldest daughter, so similar to her father in her excesses, to the second one, whose placid exterior concealed her need for special attention and who bonded more with her older sister than with her mother, to her third daughter, whom she called "the little one," and of course to her son, by four years the youngest. The Deceased landed the post of Minister of Public Health and Social Affairs two years after their son was born. At the time, who would have expected to see him become president of the country only a few years later?

But she should follow her own command: tell of her children at the outset and before all else. "Loving and Devoted Mother." A perfect title for the first chapter of the book that was unfolding in her head. The populace had never regarded her as an attentive mother. No doubt because of her austere countenance, her fixed smile, her upraised chin, and her ceremonious gestures that made so many demands, first of all on herself, but likewise on other people. As if her portrayal of first lady took precedence over every other role.

And yet, tender feelings toward her four children overflowed from her in gigantic, powerful, and unpredictable waves. The people had never wanted to view her as a mother like all others. Even when enemies tried to kidnap her children, her one and only son and her third daughter—named after her at the Deceased's insistence—no one mentioned her maternal suffering. No one seemed to understand what it meant to learn that the flesh of her flesh had skirted death, that a human form she had carried for nine months might have ended up as no more than a lifeless bundle.

Here, in this magnificent Republic of France, where she lives in exile and where, it appears, all is good, all is beautiful, because republican values prevail, there are nonetheless madmen who snatch other people's children. Perverts and sex maniacs abuse children right under the noses of law enforcement agents, right near the shopping malls where everything for the wellbeing of mother and child is available for purchase, in this country so protective of the rights of the individual. How many times have the media broadcast sobbing appeals for the return of a kidnapped child? How many posters tacked up, how many police checkpoints on the highways? How many alerts launched, in colors keyed to the level of hysteria?

Should her children have had any less importance in the grand scheme? No one thought about her despair that morning. While she and the Deceased were following the latest news, and rumors were flooding in from everywhere, while she was waiting with her heart pounding for them to bring her children back unharmed. As for those who dared to strike at her children, had they not foreseen that they would provoke her anger, frustration, and hostility? Standing next to the Deceased, who was equally enraged, she approved the planned reprisals with all her heart, as well as the measures to be taken against the guilty parties. If they had so much as laid a finger on her son, many other children would have perished. Even nailed helplessly to this bed, she felt the fury of that day surge through her limbs and turn her fingers into claws. The mothers began screaming when the Deceased blocked school dismissals and ordered the confinement of all primary, intermediate, and secondary students in their school buildings. A hair of her son's head touched and they would all have been annihilated. It was so easy to label those measures as barbaric and ruthless, whereas the Deceased had only wanted to deter further actions of the same kind and to teach the abductors a memorable lesson. To send them a clear and effective message that no attack against his children

*would be tolerated and that the culprits would be punished in
the harshest and most extreme manner.*

*All the more so because these craven individuals had at-
tacked their son! The Deceased had always wanted a son. On
the day of the little one's birth, he had approached the bed and
nervously run his hand over the newborn's head. An unforgettable Monday. Behind his glasses, his eyes seemed pensive,
almost melancholy. "He'll be a lawyer," he declared, and they
had smiled at each other, too overcome to speak.*

« »

You used to say in a voice full of sadness that you detested
the people of your island. In the face of poverty, dictatorship,
disease, and malnutrition, murky drinking water and clouds of
dust, you would murmur, "How disgraceful! To have set out
from such heights and to end up *there*." And you'd add, "The
conditions in Quisqueya bring tears to my eyes. Since we left,
everything has gotten worse."

I was only four then, you say. Still, you almost reproach
me for having forgotten the date of our permanent departure,
that Sunday in 1980, several weeks after the mournful date
that goes unmentioned. You know perfectly well you left me no
choice, Maman, since you punctuated my childhood with your
lamentations, your rage, and your pain. You made sure to tell
me about events I hadn't lived through, and you kept repeating them until my memory latched onto them. Hiding only the
circumstances of my father's death, as if to protect my childhood, though you had already contaminated it forever. Your
only daughter, a living relic of your one true love—who was
tragically killed. Me, the one for whom you chose to leave your
country, the one with whom you shared until your dying breath
the slightest events of your daily existence, the one whose life
was reduced to giving a meaning to your own.

« »

*Is it so hard to understand that a mother is attached to her
children and cannot endure anyone threatening them or mak-*

ing targets of them? Naturally, a mother must not be confused with a woman who merely opens her legs to give life and then abandons the child to its fate. For reasons of seemliness, such women claim, or out of necessity or lack of choice. Nonsense. Only adults can manage to explain away the abandonment of children. The child perceives nothing but the pain of the rejection, which burdens her all through life. It is fortunate that in our poor and miserable country, in which the Deceased did everything possible to improve the people's lot, women of that kind were not often encountered. In contrast, there was no shortage of absent fathers. Always somewhere else, running after other potential mothers and leaving behind the consequences of their promiscuity. But the women clung to those bits of flesh that had emerged from their bellies. Mothers quick to dispense slaps, spankings, and abusive language, but nonetheless present for their children, except when death stopped the carousel and plucked another victim from her ill-fated existence.

In the orphanage where she found herself one fine morning, most of the other girls were talking about their mothers, adorning them with virtues, and no one dared question the truthfulness of their fervent declarations. On Mother's Day, all of them were required to attend Mass, and the majority of the orphans, in keeping with their status, wore white ribbons as a sign of devotion to a deceased mother. She pretended to have lost her ribbon, but she had secretly crumpled it up and thrown it away. Her sisters born of different fathers disapproved, condemning her stubborn coldness toward their mother. How could she blame them for failing to understand her? The families of their respective fathers had welcomed them. But why would she have venerated a mother who had shunted her off to an orphanage at an early age? The institution had shown her no leniency. Everything had to be done correctly, perfectly, without blemish. The orphans had no right to moodiness or emotional attachments. The beds properly made, the plates washed, dried, and put away, nothing left lying around. Neither undergarments, smiles, tearstains, nor urges to smash things. She put her life on hold while awaiting her release from this sterile, tidy prison. Though miserable and wretched, she made herself the ideal

*pupil, intelligent, well-behaved, and respectful. She had to learn
patience. She did.*

*An orphanage is not a place for children whose parents are liv-
ing; parents of that sort deserve to be seen as irresponsible and
abhorrent creatures. Like that middle-class father, a brilliant
and internationally known intellectual, who got her mother
pregnant while she was working as a domestic in his family's
home. As a sordid tale, it is impossible to do better, even if
the storyline is totally unoriginal. The only advantages Odile
derived: her light-colored skin, the aristocratic contours of her
face, and the lofty stature that became legendary in national
and international press coverage. The exceptional height that
attracted the Deceased and always allowed her to appear stately
and glamorous in photos. A pity that none of her children had
inherited her beauty! But each of them resembled her in some
way, and she loved them boundlessly.*

« »

No, Maman, I can't blame you for the morbid chaos my life has
become. How could I hold you responsible when my wounds
seem so minor compared to yours?

« »

*Mothers are surely worthy of honor. The Loving and Devoted
Mother caught on very quickly to her fellow citizens' penchant
for placing maternity on a pedestal, dedicating love songs to
her, buying her brand-new furniture on New Year's Day, giving
her perfume and flowers as tokens of their gratitude. She understood it so well that she felt privileged when the populace called
her "Maman Odile." Especially at the beginning, she gratefully
accepted this nickname, which seemed to represent a commu-
nal reflex of kinship and acceptance. At the orphanage, it was
customary to evoke the family during evenings of intimate conversation, between a skimpy, unsatisfying serving of cornmeal
mush and a mug of lemongrass tea, at the hour when a defeated
hunger resigns itself to going to bed. At this moment when her
peers could no longer conceal their misery, she always turned*

quiet. She never displayed her unhappiness in a way that would cause her companions either to pity or to humiliate her. Why would she have revealed the burden that was so heavy in her memory, only to intensify her already abject shame? Instead, she watched the others expectantly await the sympathy of their audience and the illusory comfort it would bring.

Sometimes she cried in her sleep, incensed that she could not stop herself from experiencing the dream that came floating behind her closed eyelids. Blurry enough to retain its surreal character, but discernible enough to make her shudder with pain and longing. Hostage to the dream, she wept without knowing why, and submerged beneath a spate of afflictions, she was unable to stifle her sobs. Tears covered her face. An accumulation of woes, crammed together, beyond counting. She foundered beneath their weight, and her breathing came in uneven spasms. With each gasp, she descended a bit lower, toward the bottom of an abyss that was like an interminable well shaft. Then a soft, enveloping light spread through the space. Seeped into her. She inhaled and rose toward the surface. Always this hope, each time intense, marvelous. And each time she let herself be drawn in. She groped for the wall. Encountered only a void. The light passed over her indifferently. She resumed her descent toward nothingness. Two very black arms, drifting within the space, advanced toward her but did not grab hold of her. Each time, she sank to the depths of the abyss and then awoke with moist eyes. Always, she violently wiped away the tears. Certain sufferings are not to be discussed.

« »

I remember very little about the day of our departure, but I do recall the passport with its red and black cover, made of stiff, scratchy plastic. A passport bearing assumed names. Marie-Gisèle Lallemand and her four-year-old daughter, Marie-Alice, formerly Marie-Carmelle and Marie-Ange. You had prepared me well, and I was so scrawny that the immigration officers suspected nothing—even though fear glued my new name to my lips. Does my love of silence stem from that experience? I sensed myself protected from prying questions. Later on, you quickly sorted things out, regularized our papers, and obtained French nationality for me. You believed that a French passport would open doors for me, allowing me to leave the Antilles for France. You shook me out of my little girl's lethargy and disorientation so that I could adapt quickly to their school, their curriculum, and the local Creole, which was different from yours yet similar in its origins.

Even then, I retreated into silence when confronted with the taunts and rude remarks of the other children. From preschool to elementary, from middle school to high school, with my former name restored to me yet tainted with a fleeting illegality, I learned to surround myself with an impenetrable haze. When life brought too much hardship, I retreated into your memory, almost as if I wanted to return to your womb. You never understood how much I carried your country in my wounded expression, in my posture made sullen by misery. People looked my way without noticing me, and I slipped invisibly past them.

"Say, you—you come from Quisqueya. You smell like wild grass, the woods, and something else I can't place. Three hundred boat people landed in Florida last week, but dead bodies washed up on the shore. The dead ones were so bloated that no one could identify them. You think maybe you knew them? After all, they came from your country. What about you, are you one of those boat people, too? The teacher said not to ask you that, she said you came on an airplane, but we'd really like to know." When I tried to tell you about my childhood troubles, you shook your head irritably. You had seen so many horrors; my little woes seemed insignificant to you.

« »

Why should the regime have shown any mercy to conspirators? Nothing but severity could have kept the revolutionary regime in power for so long. The best course was to be unyielding and forceful when confronting an ignorant populace and a self-serving clique who were just waiting for an opportunity to seize control. Who would stop at nothing. To shoot at a child as he is leaving school? How monstrous! Then they dared to brand the Deceased and his supporters as oppressors.

She had always loathed the unjust depiction of them as ruth-less profiteers: they were doing their best to spare the people the pain and humiliation of seeing the international press, always eager to drag the country through the mud, vilify the Deceased and his cabinet. After all, how could the Western countries ever forgive or forget Napoleon's debacle, the sorry defeat of the French army in Quisqueya, and the rout of the French colo-nizers at the hands of an army of former slaves? That history remains in their hearts like a gaping wound, never to be closed. Everything serves them as a pretext for making a proud and courageous people pay for its glorious past. The Deceased un-derstood this perfectly. He didn't mince words, and he always stood up to the former colonialists, the one-time occupying power, and all those who wanted to use the country as a spring-board for their global ambitions.

But try explaining that to the plotters who craved power! He had to battle against conspiracies. The military command-ers never stopped fomenting them; likewise, in their way, the Catholic clergy, not to mention the god-awful Communists. One year the Deceased counted six foiled coups and assassina-tion attempts. In the end, however, he died in his bed! What God has done, only God can undo. The motto of the three Ds fits perfectly: the Divinity, great architect of the universe; Desravines, the supreme artisan of liberty; and of course Fabien Doréval, master builder of the New Quisqueya. One and indi-visible.

When the members of her entourage began to profess their sym-pathy and loyalty after the attempted kidnapping of her son, she refrained from telling them to go to hell. Distrusting their fearful, hypocritical, and evasive glances, she stared at them distantly and inscrutably, concealing the implacable fury which filled her and to which she clung to control her panic.

It is never wise to toy with a mother's anger. So said Ma-demoiselle Germaine, superintendent of the orphanage. In the evening, the girls would surrender to their need for human warmth, revealing their most secret fears, snuggling against one another to listen to Mademoiselle Germaine. She gorged them

on tales of wantonness and revenge that her years of embit-
tered loneliness had gradually nourished. Although dedicated
to God, Mademoiselle Germaine managed to reconcile her old
maid's piety with these very human emotions. She exuberantly
launched into her repertoire of indecorous stories, stained with
meanness and squalor, with vulgar sentiments and unbridled
passions, making a pretext of her intention to educate her poor
young orphans and prevent them from succumbing to the temp-
tations that brought glints of desire to her eyes. The girls were
not taken in. In the evening, as they lay curled up in their clean
and solitary beds, each one called to mind the image that was
the most provocative for her, the one most certain to give her
body that pleasurable tingle of venial sin.

« »

You focused all your energy on becoming familiar with our new
way of life and on using French in everyday conversation. In
Martinique, that language crept into every corner of your life,
insinuating itself into mundane exchanges in the street or marketplace. Sometimes, though, you resisted this invasion, holding fast to the Creole that you particularly wanted me to retain.
As if my clumsy stammering would bring back to me the father
you never wanted to talk about, restore you, Maman, to whole-
ness, or heal a flayed country. You used to croon very softly
in Creole, as if asking loved ones for forgiveness. You, who in
your native Quisqueya never saw white people except from a
distance, in department stores, airport counters, and televised
ceremonies, became accustomed to multiple and frequent contacts with white Frenchmen in Fort-de-France, both Zoreilles*
and visitors. You looked at them from your own particular perspective. I would have preferred that you drop your constant
comparisons between the French Antilles and your native country, but your whole existence was wrapped up in the stories you
endlessly recounted to me.

You began with the terror that overwhelmed your mother
after the attempted kidnapping of Jean-Paul Doréval, the dictator's son. I relived the scene with you, as if I had been there.

As soon as reports were confirmed of shots fired at the president's two youngest children, all mothers sprang into action. The news that students would be held in their schools spread with the dizzying speed of a catastrophe: mothers who worked in the city rushed to collect their children and warn their neighbors. Paying no attention to their appearance, many clad in slippers, the women tumbled down the hillsides, dove into taxis and vans. Men sprinted along without a care for motorists' blaring horns and the shouted rebukes of passersby. All parents wanted to retrieve their children before the blade of vengeance fell. The whole city took on a gray cast. Without really understanding the adults' fear, the children ran to keep up, their young feet tripped up by the uneven sidewalks. The luckiest parents had time to remove their daughters or sons before the enraged dictator's order reached his zealous hellhounds.

At the school of Notre-Dame du Mont-Carmel, attached to the health center of the same name, tearful mothers tried to take their children away. Sinclair, the administrator of the health center and formerly a bricklayer's assistant, had been promoted for his unswerving devotion to the revolutionary government. When mobilized by the great leader, he rushed there immediately and ordered the headmistress to detain the schoolchildren until he received confirmation that Jean-Paul and Ti Odile were out of danger. For fifteen interminable minutes, the head nurse at the center tried to persuade Sinclair to change his mind.

She was used to his headstrong whims. One Friday he'd forgotten to refrigerate the doses of anti-typhoid vaccine, and the following Monday he claimed that putting them in the freezer for a day would make them usable again, even though the outside temperatures had reached 90 degrees over the weekend. The nurse had succeeded in persuading him to discard the ampoules by mimicking his mode of thought. "Have you forgotten that Papa Fab fought against tuberculosis? He won't appreciate your putting the lives of the people's children at risk; it would be like working against the revolution."

In the same way, on this April morning in 1963, the nurse summoned all her wits and her full powers of persuasion to convince Sinclair. She invoked his ailing mother, whom she had seen one day in the chapel of Mont-Carmel. "What would she think of you if she knew you were responsible for the deaths of all these children?" Grumbling and threatening her personally with grievous punishment if an opponent of the regime should harm Papa Fab's children, Sinclair finally let the children leave.

In those days you attended a school run by the Sisters of Divine Wisdom, and your mother, no less panic-stricken than other parents, went there to find you. That same evening the cleaning woman, whose twelve-year-old daughter, Nicole, was a student at Mont-Carmel, told you of Sinclair's reaction to the attempted abduction of the Doréval children.

I tried several times to escape from your memories, or to choose the happiest ones, like those games of jacks between Nicole and you in the late afternoon. Your fingers moved quickly and precisely as you tossed the jacks and then caught them. Since the two of you were equally adept, you would take turns winning for hours at a time. I, too, tried to master the game, but I was never able to attain your level of skill, and I could see clearly that I was disappointing you. In the end, my only inheritance from you was your torment.

« »

Walled up in her silence, the Guardian of the Revolution could not rid herself of a sense of failure; ultimately, she did not succeed in imbuing her children with her vision of things, her dreams for the newly enfranchised middle class. And yet, those people's rights had to be fought for and stoutly defended. The right to an education. The right to realize their potential. The right to plant their feet with pride in a country where for too long the sole determinant of an individual's prospects had been skin color.

She had constantly witnessed the injustice of the status quo in that orphanage run by a Frenchwoman, funded by patrons from the top of the social scale, and located in a well-to-do section on the hillsides of Alexandreville. In those days Alexandreville flaunted its affluence. As proof, it sufficed to count the number of citizens with darker skin than hers. Very few, or rather, none! Peasants didn't go there except on their way down to the city with freshly picked vegetables from Karkoff and

Fancy, those villages where families who were smugly protective of their light complexions had built vacation homes, carefully sheltered from all contact with the impoverished masses. Luxurious stone houses, well-endowed with flowering shrubs and guard dogs to ward off those who might risk going there despite every indication that they were not wanted. After more than a century and a half of cohabitation in the same island nation, anyone who didn't feel the rejection would surely have to be obtuse. If you are not of the proper hue, you become invisible in certain settings. Without deliberate malice, people look right through you. Furthermore, you lose substance in your own mind, you blend into the background. You no longer exist, it's as simple as that! It's a pity that none of her children grasped the magnitude of the problem. Most of all, it's a pity that they found another way around it.

What does it matter! Despite the disgraceful failings of her own brood, she knew that a mother invests herself in each of her children and embraces the whole experience: good and bad moments, betrayal and devotion, tenderness and indifference. Yet when she was young, no hint of a sacrificial spirit marked her out for motherhood, not a drop of martyr's blood flowed in her veins. On the contrary, a determination to avenge life's disappointments and a drive to succeed possessed her constantly, outweighing all feelings of warmth or attachment. Until she found in her arms a tiny individual, helpless and at the mercy of her omnipotence, who transformed her into a she-wolf stupefied by the magnificence of her love. Astonishing even to the Deceased! She, so guarded in her affections, abandoned herself unconditionally to this feeling of adoration and self-denial that took hold of her when her first child was born and didn't lessen with any of the three that followed.

« »

Latifa insists I should see a shrink. In the beginning, she thought my nightmares were linked to the grieving process, because they started shortly after your death, but their persistence frightens her a bit. I felt so guilty after those months of estrangement from you. Also guilty for not crying, for not being able to wail with grief, for staying devastated, too crushed by the suddenness of the loss to protest out loud. But these dreams, your dreams, invade my existence both day and night. I feel drained, too bruised for modest diversions, an evening at the movies with old college classmates or an intimate dinner with a guy I like well enough to bother seeing, since it is indeed necessary from time to time to go out and to make love. Latifa says she'll take me to the shrink herself if I don't go on my own. "Things can't go on like this, honey. It's not normal." Nothing is normal. Why should my dreams hold such sway over me? In them I appear as lead actress or spectator, primary victim or simple passerby, but always, always, aware of the horror and unable to escape it. Besides your stories, you left me your notebooks covered with frenzied jottings of memorable dates, anecdotes, and passages filled with the drabness you endured yet bursting with your zeal to live. For my part, unbeknown to you, I scribbled numerous notes accumulated since adolescence, culled from my reading of works on the Doréval dictatorships, from old Quisqueyan magazines discovered at the Schoelcher Library in Martinique, from films and documentaries, and from the accounts of relatives and friends gleaned here and there. My nightmares are like hybrid monsters that restore all those things to me in a horrifying and always unexpected jumble.

1960. The student strike. You were just a child, Maman. A child fascinated by the stories of your older cousins and your big brother. More than thirty years later, I carry this load of memories folded and refolded into a thousand bloody origamis. Lives upended amid the atrocities. The sudden flarings of insurrection, the stirrings of rebellion against oppression. The irrepressible yearning for liberty.

For you, the year marked the beginning of your primary education against a backdrop of precautions and prudence. Injunctions and warnings. Discipline and rigor. Only girls were admitted to the sisters' school, where life ran up against the black-clad nuns. Covered from head to toe, their hands fingering rosary beads, the nuns crossed themselves as they passed in front of the chapel. Overwhelmed by the enforced silence of the corridors, you weren't as good at whispering as the other girls. Talking too loud was your earliest sin.

1963. A pivotal date. Year of the attempted kidnapping of the Doréval children, the ensuing reprisals, and the string of conspiracies both before and after. A mosaic of blood, crackling firearms, men in dark glasses, and children in tears. Children everywhere screaming or too appalled to make a sound, their eyes wide with horror. In one of your family albums, you showed me a photo of you in your school uniform and white socks, your braids tied with ribbons and a schoolbag in your hand. A mischievous smile on your lips, still carefree and happy, an almost defiant Marie-Carmelle who has not yet taken the airplane with me, a Marie-Carmelle I will never know.

On the bed with its whiff of approaching death is this washed-out old woman who hides her haughty expression from the world. Seeing her makes me relive your last days, Maman. Being obliged to bathe, touch, and feed her takes me back to your blighted youth and to all those memories you held tightly in your grip until the end.

« »

Notwithstanding her decision to remain in her interior world, everyday demands sometimes invaded her mind and dragged her back to this seedy nursing home where she was ending her days. So far from the sea. Then she would turn her impassive gaze on the caregiver who had dared to disturb her silence while she was deep within herself. She itched with the urge to display her annoyance and displeasure. Malevolent thoughts arose in her mind. Was it her fault that these people—the majority of them immigrants—could snag only menial jobs in those suburbs created as dumping grounds for blacks and Arabs? Was it her responsibility if their faces bore the scars of neighborhood brawls in dingy locales with pathetic names? Compound names, saints' names, with noble sonorities, yet they were bywords for instability and segregation: Épinay-sur-Seine, Clichy-sous-Bois, Neuilly-sur-Marne, Noisy-le-Sec.

She had heard stories of Quisqueyan immigrants working clandestinely, earning next to nothing, living in foul conditions,

*with a nagging, visceral fear of being deported to their home-
land. Why had they wanted so desperately to leave Quisqueya?
Spurning the Deceased's efforts to haul them out of poverty,
they had let themselves be caught in the trap of the French
Antilles or Barbados, or even worse, that of the island's other
republic. No sense of history! How could they forget the infamous massacre of Quisqueyans at the beginning of the century?
Some say nearly twenty thousand perished, others claim thirty.
And yet they persist in flocking to the border, toward the bateyes,* toward humiliation and death.*

*Why have they not adopted as their model the Deceased's
proud and uncompromising demeanor? She remembered the
time when he kept the adjacent country's great general waiting for an hour. What an affront! What delicious revenge! The
generalissimo was sweating inside his well-cut uniform. That
traitor, that man without a history, who denied his own origins.
To conceal his own mother because she was black was truly a
sign of a pathological mind. She and the Deceased spoke several
times about this neighboring head of state and his overblown
ambitions. The only good qualities the Deceased saw in him
were, first of all, his skill in at least partially foiling the plans of
the Americans, who were always interfering in other countries'
domestic affairs, and second, his sense of family. Because in all
honesty the Deceased had to admit that the generalissimo took
care of his mother even while he kept her under wraps.*

only goods
against
Americans

*On that score, the general and the Deceased resembled
one another. The family came before all else. As soon as the
Deceased had enough influence, he used it to benefit his father, Dorcas Doréval, who was named justice of the peace in
Grande-Plaine. A locality destined to give the Deceased plenty
of trouble, it would figure later in the conspiracies and intrigues.
But what did it matter whether Dorcas Doréval had been born
in Quisqueya or Martinique? The Deceased wasn't going to let
a detail like that disqualify him from the presidential contest.*

*Even before the election, as a loyal son he had helped his
father retain his pension. Or at least, to be frank about it, the
Joris brothers had looked after things. They had likewise inter-
vened to help the Deceased acquire an old pickup truck so that*

he could start a transportation business. Without their support, that would have been harder. On several occasions, the Jorises had bent over backward to do them favors. It was a shame that things had turned out as they did and that the regime had been forced to liquidate the brothers. Who would have believed it? If you can't trust such good friends, how does life make any sense? But the revolutionary government had to punish them. In such cases, personal attachments don't enter into the calculus. Gratitude is no excuse for weakness. And if someone refuses to understand this, it isn't worth belaboring the point.

Over the years, she and the Deceased were tested by several attempts to sow discord within the ruling family, to plant seeds of jealousy or dissension among the children, or to heighten the Deceased's suspicions regarding his close associates. Fortunately, she never hesitated to put her children's interests first, ahead of anyone else's. Thus, she had managed to prevent the banishment of her son-in-law, which would surely have occasioned a bruising quarrel with Marie-Danielle. To think that the Deceased had not appreciated how much she resembled him, this daughter who as a very young child would clench her fists in rage when someone stood up to her! To take excessive measures against her husband would have led directly to a falling-out with Marie-Danielle and to the estrangement of both their grandson and their second daughter, who followed her elder sibling everywhere. It would have created a permanent breach within the family. The grandmother in her could not have borne it.

An old adage says that the parents of a daughter cannot predict what animal she will bring to dine at their table. Her eyes closed and her mind intent on the still-raw memory of her humiliation, she questioned the wisdom of the proverb: a son can cause just as much parental heartache as any daughter. She could not overcome her bitterness. Events had proved her right, and though it had all happened a very long time ago, she knew she would die with the memory of the gangrenous feud between her son and herself.

It's true that the daughters have also given her their share

*of anxieties and difficulties. Especially the eldest, always quick
to challenge authority, to second-guess instructions. Yet Marie-
Danielle's regal bearing had earned her a goodly number of
admirers, some more promising than others. She welcomed
their ardor as no more than her due. In that regard, if she had
behaved in a more ingratiating manner, she could have made
more headway with that Arab. On the other hand, the Deceased, concerned about his image as a nationalist, did nothing
to facilitate things, going so far as to demand that Fakim adopt
Quisqueyan citizenship. Like father, like daughter, you'd have
to say of those two. As if it was customary for his eldest daughter to receive flowers from an Arab sheik! Each time he left the
country, he sent her some. Sheik Fakim! At least that's how
he introduced himself, and he had been treated as such, until
the day he absconded with millions of gourdes from the public
treasury. The Deceased threw a fit over it . . .*

*How would he have reacted to the wedding of his son and
the Foreigner? Would he have turned over in his grave before the
conspicuous show of luxury, the crass display of bad taste, the
resurgence of a caste who were eager to vindicate their sense
of entitlement, dragging in their wake a whole panoply of out-
moded instincts, of prejudices that had not been permanently
buried?*

<« »>

You were barely ten in 1964, the year of the "Presidency for
Life" and the grotesque, bloodthirsty antics that surrounded
it. The prearranged mob in the street, the referendum orches-
trated to a score of terror. The catechism of the revolution that
derided a people's intelligence in order to satisfy one person's
megalomaniacal cravings. "Who are Desravines, Alexandre,
and Vénérable? Desravines, Alexandre, and Vénérable are
three founders of the Nation who live on in Fabien Doréval
. . ." The persistence of my questions irritated you a little. "Did
you repeat that catechism, too, Maman? But didn't you learn
a different catechism at school when you made your first communion?"

Your memories of the following year always brought tears to your eyes because of the fate of the uncle I never knew. Jean-Édouard, your big brother! The kind of brother everyone dreams of having, the one who wipes the tears you try to hide, applies a gentle pressure to urge you forward, leaps to your aid in times of need, and smiles tenderly when you brush away his hand. You had such a gleam in your eyes when you spoke of him that I, as an only child, wanted an older brother of my own to cradle me in the solidity of his love. How envious you made me with those rare, poignant images of brief, noisy family discussions, of false quarrels, of outings to the weekend matinee at the Paramount Theater. Under Jean-Édouard's vigilance, you would turn up in your Sunday best. This was invariably the outcome of a long battle against the anxieties and restrictions of your mother, who was tormented by her fear that things could turn out badly. Sometimes your father would intervene in a gruff tone: "Let her go, they're kids, you know." He must have thought, but didn't add, "Despite the dictatorship, despite the terror." To keep you at home would be to capitulate for the umpteenth time, to admit his defeat.

As you recalled your father's throaty laugh booming in the background, you would describe those excursions as your moments of freedom. I imagine the atmosphere of those Sunday mornings with their exquisite savor of liberty, the young people clustering by gender and age, the candy sellers, the whispers, one hand brushing another, the sly winks. A band of young boys swirls around Jean-Édouard as he holds forth on mini-jazz,* the hottest new musical groups, and the pop hits of the day.

After Jean-Édouard's death, your father never laughed again. He hid behind his drink and his cigarettes, and silence filled the house.

« »

The Deceased understood that to remain in power, he had to rely on the masses, give them renewed confidence in the form of rifles, pistols, or wads of dollars, and in that way assure their loyalty. To tell the truth, it wasn't just the uneducated classes who swore fidelity to the revolution: doctors, renowned lawyers, journalists, merchants, and industrialists, dark-skinned or light, also understood where their main chance lay. For glory, power, wealth. Everyone has a weak spot. As an intelligent man, the Deceased knew how to deal with human nature. He brilliantly neutralized the student movement. He offered positions to one or another, favoring those whose academic performance left something to be desired. He successfully induced them to change sides and denounce their former comrades who were less ambitious, more courageous, or just plain unlucky.

If an individual did not yield to temptation, other means of persuasion were available, some of which might be deemed harsh, but governing a nation entails sacrifice. As their great friend Lambert Chambral used to say, "A good Dorévalist is always ready to murder his children, the children to eliminate their parents." Nor did the Deceased hesitate to set aside his personal feelings for the collective good. She was thinking of her sister Clara's husband, Léonard Daumier, who was executed during the 1960s. Fiery and idealistic, he had fought stubbornly against Loiseau in 1946. The Deceased counted on him in the very beginning for speeches and other services, but Léonard refused to abandon his leftist views; like bones stuck in his throat, they distorted his behavior. Endangering the common good. Fortunately, Clara was able to divorce him quickly. They had done everything to spare her this ordeal, but it became necessary to resolve the situation. That's what it means to be a revolutionary: to make the necessary sacrifices without hesitation. To pay the price, whatever it may be. In fact, she wondered whether the revolution didn't demand the same level of sacrifice and selflessness as motherhood.

« »

I don't know why I'm so affected by the death of an uncle who passed away long before I was born, but I feel it like a keen and haunting ache. Like a song heard by chance that can never be recaptured. Perhaps because your voice betrayed such depths of dejection that I had no choice but to descend with you into the pit of hell. Waiting in the early morning with your whole family in the entry hall of the military headquarters, and later at the perimeter of Fort Décembre. To recover the swollen corpse. The silent anguish of your mother, who, the same month, suffered her first attack of high blood pressure and lost what little remained of her zest for living. Your father choking back his tears and swallowing his pride in order to gain the right to bury his eldest son, a student in his preparatory year of law school, because any hint of indignation could provoke dreadful consequences. The responsibility for the family's survival rested on the shoulders of a man who'd been honest and proud all his life and who now felt a sudden urge to kill. And you, Maman, the abandoned little sister, sensed the impossibility of asking questions, for the voices of the adults were brutally silenced. The family cut short the funeral to protect the corpse from any kind of assault. A grief sentenced to concealment. In the obscurity of the bedroom, or in the nauseating odor of the latrines, a grimy desolation, stained with shame, frustration, and rage. A mute distress, life reduced to a scorched earth, never to be as it was.

In a rare anticlerical impulse, your father emerged briefly from his despondency to enroll you in a nonreligious, coeducational school for the three years following elementary school. It was his final intervention before handing on to your mother the responsibility for all decisions concerning the family now bereft of its eldest son. That was the year of your first love. You admitted this to me with regret in your voice, as if you were somehow reproaching yourself for the crush you had on one of your classmates. His name was Richard. A fellow student entwined your names in the center of a heart drawn prominently on the blackboard. You indignantly erased it, as if you had lost the right to fall in love. As if you were renouncing all aspirations of happiness. You were not yet fifteen.

Nevertheless, you kept a diary until 1968. Every evening you retreated to a corner of the living room to scribble your thoughts in it, everything that was passing through your head. All the things that couldn't be said out loud. One evening your mother wanted to read it. "Just to know," she said. "After all, you're only a child, Marie-Carmelle." That diary was your open door, your wings, your shallow breathing, the ballroom where you whirled endlessly. How could you have shared it? You threw the notebook into the latrines. Your mother wouldn't have understood any of it.

1969. Some peasants rebelled in a little village in the center or the south. The flames of revolt blazed for hours on end before being snuffed out. Dozens of confirmed deaths. Hundreds missing, both notable figures and anonymous ones. Those who could leave the country did so. Those who stayed, always the greater number, fought, kept silent, bore the wounds of their daily life in their own diverse ways. At least ten students from your class emigrated before the end of the school year. The director quickly put the empty benches into storage. His establishment could not afford to be seen as a breeding ground for dissidents, a training center for exiles.

The Corbières, a family as old as the community, also left. Three married sisters, their husbands, and their children, all living under the same roof. I don't know whether I truly remember this immense house with its courtyard and garden or if I imagine it from what you told me about it. They came often, especially the two youngest sisters, to visit your mother at the end of the day. The three women would chatter over a cup of coffee or herbal tea. You used to play at their feet while eavesdropping on their conversations, stocking your memory with bland-seeming remarks to be deciphered later. Sometimes your mother would signal you to go play somewhere else. You knew then that they were going to broach a touchy subject: a sister's unfaithful husband or a political question. You dragged your feet in hopes of catching a few snatches of conversation, but a stern look from your mother sufficed to compel your obedience. The women's laughter or whispers followed you, and you imagined stories full of salacious details and intriguing dilemmas. With their children and their husbands, the three sisters left for the United States, one after the other, like grapes plucked from a bunch by an invisible but inexorable hand. Soon none of the family was left except an old aunt who until her death spent her days waiting for the mail to arrive.

You barely mentioned the major events of the following year. Somehow your near silence terrified me even more.

1970. Silence weighs still more heavily on Port-du-Roi. Daily life hurries along, but large areas of the city are shrouded in terror.

You insist on leaving to join your cousins who emigrated to Montreal at the beginning of the year. In their letters, they discuss their university studies, the snow, and the TV shows. They mourn Jean-Édouard's memory, but they mention him less and less, already far removed from a state of bereavement. You envy them and come close to disliking them. Your Aunt Élise promises to take care of everything: you could finish secondary school in Montreal and go on to university there. To everyone's great surprise, the Canadian consulate rejects your visa application. In any case, your parents refused to leave the country. Knowing you as I do, Maman, you would not have abandoned them. As time went by, you said, you stopped thinking about it. I will never know if, deep inside, you regretted staying. But you always asserted that destiny reigns over everyone. You met Papa. In due course I was born. Me, Marie-Ange, your very own angel.

1971. You go down to take the exam for your secondary school diploma, along with thousands of other candidates. It's the year of the dictator's death. In the social sciences test, one of the optional questions calls for comment on a famous statement of Fabien Doréval: "One of the fundamental missions of the Quisqueyan elite is to lift up the social level of the common people so that the masses can follow the elite in their ascent toward the light." Sensibly enough, you opt instead to analyze the famous Southern War, in which the partisans of Alexandre opposed those of Kristof. You later learn, however, that the candidates who chose to discuss Doréval's pronouncement automatically received thirty bonus points.

« »

An incident returned to gnaw at her, even though she thought it had been erased from her memory after so many years. Few

people knew it, but she used to love listening to Edith Piaf.
That captivating voice, capable of translating any song into an
avalanche of strong sensations. A journey out of the self. An
intense pleasure, with no consequences except unbridled happi-
ness and a little sigh when the sound of the voice ceases, though
it can be brought back with a slight movement of the hand. On
one occasion in their rather rundown lodgings, long before the
presidency, she was listening to Piaf on an antiquated turntable
bought from a friend who was moving away. She was spell-
bound by that voice, and the final notes of La vie en rose *had*
just filled the room where she had taken refuge, alone and free.
While she was delicately setting the needle on the turntable to
hear the song again, two of her daughters burst in with a saga
of broken dolls and taunting words. Of petty bickering. Her
hand twitched, and the needle skidded across the record with a
screech, marring it forever. Ruining one of her favorite songs.
Naturally, she later obtained other recordings of Edith Piaf, but
at that particular moment she was livid with rage. She glared at
her children without saying a word, and a violent impulse to be
rid of them surged within her.

Today, old and bedbound, she finds herself alone. She knows
we are always alone at the end of life, even when relatives are
holding our hand, even when those who love us are shedding
genuine tears. We must confront death all alone. There's no
longer any way to hide behind plans, intentions, or dreams. It's
necessary to look at the life behind us and say good-bye to it.
We can pretend otherwise, but what good would it do? Along
the way, illusions and self-deception help us to continue, but at
the end of the road, they become useless masks that we must
discard, for whether we like it or not, the flesh is laid bare and
revealed for what it is.

« »

In spite of myself, I can't stop blaming your death on that feeble
octogenarian, a half-senile nursing home patient. I realize that
the leap is illogical, since I am, after all, an intelligent young
woman with excellent training. I have a degree in communi-

cations and cultural studies. As you repeated to me so many
times, I drift along in this miserable job "until I find another
more suited to my qualifications." But in spite of all the rational
arguments I wield against myself, I see this impotent patient as
an evildoer. Responsible in some measure for the shadows that
enveloped your life.

You were only forty-seven, Maman. The fact that people
under fifty can die of heart attacks does not lessen my despair.
That vile scourge is the same one that dealt an early blow to the
dictator but spared him until striking him down for good eleven
years later.

I wonder what would have happened if Doréval had succumbed to the first attack. How many lives would have been
spared, how many families would not have experienced the
disappearance of a brother, a cousin, a daughter? How many
nightmares would no longer have their reason for being? Like
running a film backward, I take the liberty of reworking history: I restore life to the young man gunned down one rainy
evening because a Tonton Macoute* wanted to kiss the man's
fiancée; I return a smile to the careworn face of the mother who,
for six years until her death, went to the police headquarters
every morning to inquire after her two sons who had been arrested for their communist views. Humbly, I restore the dignity
of his funeral to Claude Joris, candidate for the presidency at
the same time as Fabien Doréval; I rehabilitate the image of this
ceremony that became a scene of horror when men armed with
machine guns sprayed the floral wreaths with bullets and dis-
persed the dead man's friends, relatives, and sympathizers who
had come to pay him final homage. Like a sculpted Madonna,
I restore calm and peace to the Church of the Sacré-Coeur and
quietude to the assembled mourners. Solemnly, I return the stolen body to the Joris family. Serenely, I cover the walls of the
city in blue to hide the stains of the blood spattered there with
no regard for aesthetics, and I transform the huge prison of infamous name into a massive history museum. Fort Décembre,
bastion of shame, of ravaged corpses, crippled backs, mangled
fingers, and broken hearts. I rededicate it as a place of com-

memoration for the victims, the martyrs, for all those who are
remembered, but above all for those men and women who are
never spoken of. Always more numerous. The anonymous mul-
titude so often remains invisible to the eyes of posterity. But
even on days of unaccustomed boldness, I don't dare confront
the fateful date for fear of implicitly undermining your story.
Your taboos bind me to the transmitted memory and override
my own recollections. My absent father remains irretrievably
dead, an unknown in my eyes, in spite of the lovingly preserved
photos and the sketchy allusions you reluctantly offered.

In any case, I tell myself that even if the tyrant had not survived his first heart attack, he would still have accounted for an
impressive number of crimes. In less than two years in power, he
had already established violence as a means of control and de-
terrence against any and all attempted opposition. I can quickly
dredge up certain facts that have become an integral part of my
memory. First of all, the failed attempt to overthrow the regime
during the summer of 1958. Once captured, all the conspirators, both Quisqueyan and foreign, were put to death. Doréval
seized the occasion to create his Presidential Guard, purge the
armed forces, and eliminate several enemies, real or imagined.
Among those massacred were the Joris brothers, whose principal crime resided squarely in their being related to Claude
Joris, a former presidential candidate who at the time could not
be found. A despicable act, a carefully contrived charade that
fooled no one on that August day. The corpses of Clifford and
Duquesne Joris placed on the highway like conspirators caught
in their own trap. Flagrantly staged, a deed of primal simplicity
and savage cruelty. Two men actually murdered in their beds,
without trial or defense. The entire family of the former presidential candidate would become victims of Doréval's thrusts.
Then the carnage that made me wet my bed every night for a
week after you described it: the decimation ordered by Doréval
to solidify his accession to power. Two nights in June, bloody
and hallucinating. Under the glow of searchlights, thousands of
people shot down by troops commanded by Carabine Cabral.
An onslaught against the slums. The bodies spirited away. The

streets hosed down. Two crimson nights, followed by so many days of silence.

I wonder if someday I'll be able to free myself from the forlorn and agonizing shell in which you raised me. When I look at the figure stretched out on the bed, I can't let go of my hostility, because I'm afraid that dejection will take its place and leave me with no defense against despair.

TWO

THE FIRST LADY AND THE SCHOOLGIRL

*She would have needed an abundance of peace and quiet to
put her thoughts in order, but she knew intuitively that the circumstances were not favorable. She would have liked to have
the power to punish the people who never stopped pawing her,
manhandling her bones and flesh until they felt almost liquefied,
or pulverized into clay beneath their fingers. Didn't they know
who they were dealing with? The doctors were concealing her
identity, but she suspected that her secret had leaked out quite
a while ago. She detected an element of scorn in certain looks,
as well as the rabid curiosity of more than one person. She had
spent three-quarters of her life in close proximity to a pair of
bulging eyes that were capable of reducing the steeliest adver-
saries to soggy mush, so ordinary malice bored her profoundly.
In her present situation—half dead, only halfway lucid—no one
could do her any real harm. The time for vengeance had passed;
they should have thought of it sooner. They should have done
a better job of organizing those ludicrous plots that never went
anywhere. After each abortive attempt, the Deceased's ire was
boundless. That was how they had consolidated their power.
Who would have imagined that the rather scrawny orphan girl
would enjoy a thirty-year reign as the most powerful woman in
the country? She shoved back into the crevices of her memory
the infuriating episode when the Foreigner—her son's grasping
wife—tried to pass herself off as first lady. As if our country
forgot its agony that easily.*

*No one—neither supporters nor opponents—thought the re-
gime would last. Everyone was expecting it to be toppled in the
month following the inauguration. They had failed to consider
the Deceased's intellect. Among his greatest qualities were his*

*powers of observation. During the election campaign and well
before, he had followed the political process, its upheavals, the
low blows, the acts of brute force, the backstabbing, the palace
coups. In the evenings he would often sit in meditation near the
kerosene lamp, scrawling a few notes. During those times, he
barely spoke, even to her. She left him alone to mull over their
future. She recognized, as she had to, that great minds need
silence.*

*Meanwhile, she, too, was pondering. Over the years, they
had formed the habit of communicating that way, beyond
words. Sometimes, reality would float between them, like a
great bubble waiting to be shaped in conformity with their
conception of the world. How she loved the euphoric rush that
power gave them! More intoxicating than the flesh that swells,
throbs, and explodes. She could forgo her carnal desires, disre-
gard their enticements, and fall into oblivious slumber, but the
mind addicted to power never tires of it. The Deceased used to
organize orgies of power. For the two of them, power was more
exhilarating than their naked bodies.*

<< >>

"I vow before God and this nation that I will be its zealous
and unyielding guardian. May this flag forever wave beneath
the azure sky to remind all Quisqueyans . . ." The words pour
from my memory while I effortlessly lift the old woman's legs
to change the sheets. Anyone would have thought I was the one
who had been required to repeat the pledge of allegiance every
day at school for years on end.

I still admire your storytelling talents, Maman, even if your
stories usually dealt with gruesome subjects. I can easily see
you as a young student racing to get through the schoolhouse
door before the bell rings, so as not to miss the flag salute.
When a student arrived late, all eyes converged on her. Could
her tardiness be a deliberate ploy to avoid swearing fidelity to
the revolution and its leader? Immediately, the latecomer made
a show of bellowing out the words louder than anyone else, in
case a classmate would have the unfortunate idea of mention-

ing the incident at home. All parents took pains to teach their
children that any action viewed as subversive would spark re- *threats*
prisals against the entire family. Not even the babies would be
spared, as was the case for the Sansarin family, the Boisronds,
Marthe's grandson, and the corner shopkeeper whose daughter,
it seemed, belonged to the Quisqueyan Communist Party. At
your house, Maman, after Jean-Édouard's death, all mention of
the PPPL*—the leftist party he flirted with—filled the air with
an oppressive heaviness. Above all, everyone knew better than
to give voice to any acronym beginning with *P* or containing a
C. They also knew better than to utter the word "communist"
even in the suffocating odor of the latrines. They were careful
not even to think it, and they squelched it under the soles of
their shoes so that it could never reach their lips. To prevent
slip-ups, they instilled fear in their children and initiated them
into the cult of silence.

In front of guests or new domestic help, conversations cen-
tered on dull, trite topics that were tiresome but safe. "As it turns
out, England will host the World Cup this year." "Yes, my son
was promoted to the next grade." "Did you go to Ferdinand's
daughter's wedding? I understand the bride was ravishing. It's
a pity that . . ." And the flow of words suddenly stops, for how
can the speaker openly observe that the father's appointment
as head of the national lottery coincided with a phenomenal
upsurge in the family's wealth? Or that the wedding served to
showcase their recently acquired fortune? That they are among
the regime's most diehard supporters? That their former friends
are afraid of them and that the smiles of those around them are
so strained you can hear their teeth grinding? The words stick
in the throat. The truth can do too much harm. In the privacy
of the bedroom, whispers are no longer limited to intimate acts;
they become survival mechanisms for escaping the prying ears
that can penetrate the thickest walls.

« »

As soon as the Deceased's candidacy was formally announced,
Odile assumed the bearing of a first lady, dignified and reserved.

That suited her character well. She had always deemed it neces-
sary to keep a reasonable distance between herself and others.
She hadn't the least desire to expose her emotions or be univer-
sally beloved. Better to be respected or simply feared! She em-
braced quite naturally the role of an imposing and prideful first
lady. Proud, an adjective she had long coveted. As a child, she
repeated it in combination with words like "youth" and "his-
tory" in patriotic songs learned on the school benches. Even
then, she had wanted to snatch it and graft it onto her identity,
to replace her family name with that attribute. She used to re-
peat the pleasing sequence of sounds, rolling them around in
her mouth. Odile Savien the Proud, Odile the Proud: that was
how she secretly defined herself. That was how she would like
history to immortalize her. Odile the Proud. To compensate for
all those days that had hung worryingly open, all those glances
dripping with disdain, all the rejections conveyed by a blandly
dismissive gesture of the head or hand.

<< >>

I stretch out and fold back the octogenarian's limbs one after
the other, to prevent bedsores. Through the gap between her leg
and the bleached-out cotton of her hospital gown, my eyes meet
the old lady's for a fleeting second, and her supposed dementia
seems suspect to me. Could she be more lucid than she lets
on? After all, I should mistrust such a vain and false creature,
fully capable of adopting this subterfuge and concealing herself
behind her leathery skin. Suddenly an indistinct, yet giddying,
idea tantalizes my drowsy mind. Without taking my eyes off the
face that has reverted to blankness, I mechanically pull up the
sheets. Had the time for action arrived? The time to do honor
to my father's memory and to yours, too, Maman? To the enno-
bling image of your big brother, the young uncle I never knew.
Maybe I have found here the opportunity to renew my life, to
make a remarkable break with my past, to take charge of it
and move beyond it? Maybe this is to be my path? Maman,
you often said that coincidences existed only to challenge us to
combat them or dare us to make the most of them.

« »

How annoying she was, that girl who was attending to her, while at the same time looking daggers at her! She couldn't complain to management, since the employee was performing her duties competently. Nevertheless, the young woman was bristling with animosity, even if she wasn't saying anything unpleasant or making any aggressive or overtly hostile moves. Perhaps the young woman is afraid? How gratifying to be able, even in her current helpless state, to provoke unprompted feelings of fright! She would not have thought such contentment possible so many years after her departure from the country. Such a long time since they'd been driven from power—through the fault of the Foreigner, who had never been able to control herself. Stretching her luck until it ran out. And Odile, in the dead of night, with her little band of deposed followers, like banished wrongdoers. Enduring the dull, menacing catcalls, she stepped forward under escort but without the honors due her rank as first lady. Keeping her head erect and her chin raised, as in the multiple photos of the couple when she and the Deceased would pose for posterity. Even in front of such a pitiless audience, she wasn't going to flinch during this final performance in her native land. The photographers' bulbs flared insolently. The high representatives of the "friendly" countries, always present at crucial moments, were hovering nearby. In front of her, "the Heir," her son, who had never learned to project a stature equal to his father's—she had to admit it in her heart of hearts—was advancing toward the cameras. At his side was the Foreigner, her hair wrapped in a turban. Just then the reality of the situation struck Odile violently. Her steps suddenly became so heavy! Not a shred of physical fear, but the anguish of leaving for good twisted her innards. When she approached the airplane, her bearing loftier than ever, she suddenly felt her legs balk at exile. To leave in such a manner, what a deplorable shame! And yet, no trace of a tear at the corners of her eyes. Elegant and seemingly unruffled to the end, despite the wrenching pain of her imminent and inescapable departure.

Out on the tarmac at that moment, a fresh breeze rustled the folds of her skirt, reminding her of Alexandreville at sunrise. The famous 4:00 a.m. masses when the orphans processed two by two to the nearby chapel, their faces still masked in drowsiness. The special atmosphere of the moment hushed all the chatter. "Even if you hear steps behind you, don't turn around. That's how the devil steals the souls of the careless ones." The still-cool predawn air, coupled with their nervousness, made the girls shiver deliciously, and they squeezed their arms around their sweaters, gifts from the high society ladies to the orphans. None of them would risk a backward glance. The last stars still lingered, but already, like a promise, the first rays of sunlight infiltrated the darkness. Still only half-awake, the girls sat through the Latin mass, letting themselves be lulled by the monotony of the ritual, taking communion by force of habit. They were already looking forward to the return journey, the fresh and always exquisite radiance, redolent with scents and colors. The velvety yellow of the cornmeal mush spiced with nutmeg, the little loaves taken straight from the oven and carried at arm's length in wicker baskets. The hot coffee served up by devout ladies on the church steps, in repentance for some persistent sin or out of simple generosity. The return trip evolved into a pleasant stroll, at once bracing and stimulating . . . Why were those images coming to mind and making her departure even more harrowing as she approached the airplane specially chartered for her family and herself on that February morning in 1986?

And yet, they had begun so well. September 1957. Of course, the other candidates were bustling around and making noise, but a great many men and women believed in the Deceased's platform. His oft-stated objective of creating a more just society. Too many capable and available individuals had been rejected by the preceding regimes. Nurses, accountants, diplomats, doctors, lawyers, along with military men, their talents wasted because they didn't meet the primary criterion of certain administrations: a lighter complexion, closer to that of the former colonial masters and of the recent occupying power. Ah, yes!

The American occupation had reinforced all the old prejudices. *class*
The middle class, small in number and passably prosperous,
was eager for change, especially after having tasted Vénérable's
reforms, but he had let himself be ambushed. And that Pierre-
Albert in his great general's regalia let himself be manipulated
by opportunists who came back to reclaim their traditional
place at the seat of power. A strange kind of iron fist! It's to
him that we owe the return of the light-skinned crowd and their
nominee, a certain Luc Dessau, an aristocrat who was intent on
placing himself in opposition to the Deceased. But the common
people quickly unmasked the usurpers. They took to the streets
to celebrate the victory of the man who had relentlessly battled
tuberculosis in the backcountry, shoulder to shoulder with the
peasants, while others were busy enriching themselves.

At the first press conference after the election, Fabien's intellect was on full display. She remembered the verve with which
he had fielded the journalists' questions, as if he had been doing
it all his life. "United and indivisible in the face of the nation's
enemies. We mustn't choose between the colors of the flag, but
reunite them to symbolize our oneness." The point is that the
Deceased knew how to speak, and his inimitable voice transformed his words into elemental truths. The agrarian masses,
the working classes, salt of the earth, leavening of the national
output. He knew how to rally them, set them parading in ranks
of blue uniforms beneath the midday sun. "One, two, three,
four, for our land, native land, let's march for the nation, to the
beat of the speeches and the thud of the rifle butts." Besides,
how—except with firmness—could one control that mob of illiterates, those victims of malnutrition and oafishness? They
needed an enlightened leader who had their interests at heart.
Sometimes you have to rely on military units capable of using
force. The end justifies the means. Thus, at the very beginning, *use of force*
General Carabine Cabral, with his swiftness of action, his me-
thodical mind, and his shock troops, was amply necessary. The
Deceased had not wavered for a second before calling on the
general's services. Later on, he got rid of him. The army has to
be watched constantly. The officers detest obeying a civilian,
even when the latter is president of the Republic. Just recently,

the little priest* experienced that to his detriment. They didn't hesitate to offer him a nicely packaged coup d'état.

When, on the orders of David Fédéré, the rabble began to surge through the streets, set the country on fire and commit acts of mayhem, those fledgling revolutionaries shouted, "Kill them all!" A steamroller with no sense of history. Tens of thousands of barefoot beggars rioting in the streets. The Deceased judged it essential to oppose them with an even more powerful force. Bombs were exploding, strikes breaking out. The country was about to dissolve in chaos. They all made the mistake of underestimating Papa Fab, as the peasants had taken to calling him during the campaign against tuberculosis. Since he was cleansing the countryside of the lethal disease with the same effectiveness as the famous American detergent Fab—then being sold in little blue boxes—Fabien quite naturally became Papa Fab.

Contrary to the mistaken belief of some, the self-effacing, laconic physician had not suddenly metamorphosed into a wily politician. Those who made that error saw a physical transformation in him, brought about by his awareness of power. They invented a psychological type to which the Deceased supposedly belonged—yes, she had read those books that everyone used to cite—and misapplied a simplistic model to an extraordinary man. In truth, the Deceased had simply been biding his time. At the right moment, he deployed all his advantages, including his long-standing connections and the lessons he drew from his analyses. Some politicians, impetuous and overeager, hurl themselves against brick walls and self-destruct. Others, like Fabien Doréval, possess the intelligence to wait patiently, observe closely, and act at the opportune time.

« »

For the first time in a long while, I suddenly feel as young as my twenty-three years. I'm becoming bold and bouncy, infused with an unaccustomed touch of vibrancy. I would have loved to have a similar image of you in your youth. A young woman conscious of her body and her attractiveness. You were beautiful, Maman. In that group photo of your philosophy class, a sly little expression on your lips, but a brooding sadness in your eyes, a fatalism so excruciating that it pains me to look at you. You and your classmates were all so young, I can't imagine your daily life with repression all around you. In that capital city I don't really know, having left it when I was too little to remember anything but tiny, inconsequential things: the church bells pealing at daybreak, the aroma of an almond cracked open to expose its tender, perfumed meat, the image of a little girl on a Sunday morning, with gleaming shoes and blue ribbons in her hair. How does anyone keep her own likeness in her mind's eye like an untaken photo framed in a lens?

I want to imagine you as a merry and frivolous girl, in the company of other easygoing and free-spirited young people, brimming with ideas and dreams, sensitive and impatient, happy and enthusiastic about their lives. Not the doleful and defeatist remnant they became, tramping furiously through puddles of coagulated blood, facing the barred doors of the young people's associations, the upended chairs of the film clubs and libraries. Standing before shelves of books whose titles have been condemned as subversive. Reading underground poems that someone slipped them on the sly. Circulating in hushed tones the snatches of good news they only half-believed.

"*Allons, enfants de la patrie, le jour de gloire est arrivé. Aux armes, Citoyens . . .*" I was repeating *La Marseillaise*, the French national anthem, with the other students, but in the depths of my heart, like a flower whose colors dance incessantly in the eyeballs, the words of the other anthem would come back to surprise me: "For the flag, for the homeland, our past cries out to us . . ." With my little Antillean classmates, I learned the names of great waterways on the far side of the Atlantic: the Loire, the Dordogne, the Charente. Meanwhile, lonely and threatened, the great Lenglesou of Quisqueya would flow blue in my reveries. I would memorize the principal departments of France, cite the names of its chief cities: Lyon, Rennes, Grenoble, Toulouse, Paris; recite the exploits of Joan of Arc, immerse myself in the Carolingian and Capetian dynasties, grow mildly excited about the storming of the Bastille, survey the First and Second World Wars. And in the recesses of my memory, in a whisper, your country's history would invade my imagination. I took part in the slave revolts, shouted myself hoarse at the side of Desravines, scaled the crest at Jean-Jacques, and shared a horse with the legendary François la Mort. I fell off the horse and got back on: grenadiers, to the assault! To die for the homeland is glorious. Bayonet in hand, I would become Brigitte the warrior, sewing the young nation's flag with Cécile Fanon and bursting with pride amid the bursts of mortar shells.

Your country's geography imposed its maps and contours on me. Ouadamire, in the northwest, a stone's throw from the border, a troubled area that gave the dictator a jolt when he commanded them to bring him the head of a dissident colonel. Cap Créole and the majestic outline of the citadel built by the great king. Jémanie, where children were bayoneted to death by uniformed men. Cavalier/Doréville, its name chosen to commemorate the great champion of national independence. Port-du-Roi and its vast cemetery, where the public execution of two dissidents on that November day in 1964 cast an even darker pall than the traditional Day of the Dead.

You would always describe that horrific episode with your eyes closed, as if you were seeing it again in your mind's eye. A day that lingers in the memories of a good many people, adults and schoolchildren, men and women, young and old. Lionel Dubois and Marc Noisin, two members of the rebel group called "The Thirteen," captured and condemned without trial. A mulatto and a black, victims together of the ultimate infamy. The government had ordered a massive turnout for the execution of the two men, guilty of having dared to defy the dictatorship. Elementary school pupils, middle and high schoolers, university students, and government workers were let out early to watch the spectacle, which in addition would be televised and rebroadcast so many times that no one could avoid seeing the bullet-riddled corpses. Your parents, following the example of many others, kept you at home. But how could they keep you from imagining the grisly atmosphere that hung over the city, the nausea experienced by so many spectators, the murderous jeers of the Dorévalists elated at their opponents' punishment, the horrified silence that paralyzed the onlookers and froze even the sky?

Without your parents' knowledge, Jean-Édouard, recently graduated from high school, slipped away from the family home to witness the executions. Fascinated in spite of himself, impelled by a need to act in some as yet undetermined way. When he returned, still shaken by the violence of the scene, he shut himself up in his bedroom. You went to him there—and in this, Maman, I clearly recognize your persuasive powers—you practically forced him to tell you everything, though I wonder if you didn't regret it afterward. He told the story in short sentences, with great swaths of silence that even you didn't dare interrupt. In a dreary, ragged voice, in which you could hear the curtness of the order to fire that snapped out like a horse whip, the volley of rifle shots, the dull thud of the recoiling bodies. His voice quavered with astonishment and pride as he spoke of the condemned men's defiance in the face of their executioners. His eyes glowed with admiration like the gunfire flashing in the chaos. The gob of spit flung in the face of one of the killers— had he actually seen it or merely heard the crowd murmuring about it? What did it matter?

He gave you the precious gift of a fury stronger than fear, the invaluable heritage of dignity and courage. His account finished, Jean-Édouard began to tremble. As his chest heaved with sobs, you snuggled against him. So many years later, always at that moment in the story, I in turn would huddle against you, awaiting the consequences of that tragic day, the one on which your big brother, suddenly an adult, had made his decision. Only much later did you understand.

« »

Anyone who read the newspapers after 1986—as she had done from time to time, just to nurture her anger!—would inevitably believe that all of Quisqueya's adversity was attributable to the family's thirty years in power, and above all to the Deceased's fourteen-year reign. The written history still exists, however, and the documents cannot be silent forever. She used to wish fervently that one day the public, and especially the young, would understand the reasons for the regime's actions. To lead a country is a sacred mission that calls the head of state to be deeply attentive to its transcendent interests in a spirit of sublime humanism. She would have liked so much for the young people to read and reread The Autobiography of a Third World Leader *and steep themselves in the vision of a man who sacrificed his life for his country. Anyone who understood the pitiable state of decay in which they had found the country would appreciate their efforts to remedy it. They enjoyed wide support, too—as on the occasion when Fabien was caught up in the enthusiasm of the crowd and agreed to shoulder the burden of the presidency for life. What a grave responsibility! And more than anything, what valor!*

But the smear campaign began well before their fall from power, aimed at systematically obscuring the impact of the Dorévalist revolution on the youth of Quisqueya and its role in improving the living conditions of the rural masses, who have too often been left behind. Still, the Deceased never let himself be thrown off balance by such tactics. Even in the most desperate hours, he proved equal to the challenge, never hesitating to don his simple soldier's uniform to accompany the armed forces, the VSN,* and the countless Dorévalist units from the mountains and plains.

The strain of recalling the Deceased's exact words, the linchpin of her memories, enfeebled her still more. She didn't try to resist, even in her mind, the progressive weakening of her limbs. She let herself be lifted up by competent and impersonal hands. So different from the pampered care she'd been entitled to receive as first lady. She used to adore the massages. At first, however, she had rejected this treatment, which she felt as an intrusion, an affront to her privacy and modesty. Then, gradually, she had adapted to it. Had experienced it as a symbol of her new power. A singular sensation: to feel herself at someone's mercy and yet to retain control. To let a stranger's hands make contact with her skin, smooth it delicately, knead it to the point of causing pain, while a mere gesture or raised eyebrow from her could regulate the pressure of the fingers on her back. To let makeup be applied to her face, to turn her head to the right or left like a top under the guidance of a stranger's hand, then to command that everything be wiped clean if she didn't like the result. Yes, she had undoubtedly taken to those privileges with great relish, she who had spent her childhood in fear of what each new day might bring. Only those who have lived in hidden dread of a hollow stomach at day's end, in constant apprehension of a future looming without prospects, can appreciate the peace of mind that affluence brings. And yet, she had always observed the norms, had always behaved as a worthy and respectful first lady. Hadn't Fabien said as much in his dedication to the one he called "his courageous nurse, the tireless companion of his nights of reflection . . . witness to victories and defeats, to hours of hope and discouragement . . . "? She had adopted the persona that corresponded with her rank and functions. She had never brought shame on the country.

« »

What could explain all the misfortunes that seemed to escape God's benevolence? Your Catholic education and your child-like docility posited wrongs to be atoned, sins buried deep in your subconscious. Surely you were not alone in seeking a pro-found reason for the horror that was enveloping you, a logic by which you could expand the peaceful moments—those not surrounded by a menacing aura—into long-lasting truces. You had to discover the ancestral sins that justified the tragedies. Or the continuing offense that was prompting your God to act so harshly toward your country, your friends, and your family. Otherwise, how could you account for the death of your big brother, your parents' despondent whispers, the increasingly dismal days, all the canceled celebrations, the friendships that were growing harder and harder to maintain?

As you grew older, you managed to lay aside your little girl's infractions like so much petty filching. You forgot the juicy in-sults learned from schoolmates and domestics, which you par-roted with a gusto tempered only by your fear. You discounted the urges to run away, the carnal desires and indecent thoughts,

your impish fingers inside your cotton panties. "For your pen-
ance, say ten Hail Marys and five Acts of Contrition." That was
how the parish priest, an old Breton nostalgic for the mists of
his birthplace, resolved the guilty feelings of his flock. But the
novenas and litanies failed to console you.

During your adolescence, you thought you had found an explanation for all the suffering. Once, with a touch of embarrassment, you told me how one of your father's great-aunts showed
up one day and took Jean-Édouard and you into a completely
dark cottage for a strange ceremony. At the time, you had just
turned six, and Tante Yvonne insisted on placing both of you
under the protection of the family *loas** at all costs, because
of a premonition, a terrifyingly vivid dream in which a raiding
party of zombies tried to kidnap Jean-Édouard.

Your mother refused to attend the ritual. Your father accompanied you and your brother without opening his mouth
to express his incredulity. He couldn't disobey Tante Yvonne,
the elder sister of his deceased grandmother. She was the family's medium, the one who received messages from the dead,
the one whose visits plunged the children, and with them the
entire household, into a flustered and troubled state. I imagine
many Quisqueyan families still have a similar individual in their
midst, a presumed channel of the ancestral powers, a seer to
whom everyone defers, or against whom the family skeptic one
day rebels, out of fear, wounded feelings, or both. You wondered for a long time if all your calamities didn't stem from
the family's submission to Tante Yvonne's beliefs. The cryptic
incantations and the dank odor of the crumpled, slimy leaves
with which Tante Yvonne and her plump, quiet assistant slath-
ered both Jeanjean's body and yours have long symbolized for
you the abominable sin.

Jeanjean. I can still hear the warm and melancholy affection
in your voice when you call your big brother by his nickname.
I picture the mischievous look that lasts only a second, and
your lips that purse wistfully just afterward, as if you are only
then noticing that he is gone. Taken from you so young, and so
brutally. All of Tante Yvonne's magic spells and occult ceremonies came to nothing. Just like those of your mother and other

devotees in the neighborhood. Neither rituals, candles, meals made from decapitated chickens, nor Latin canticles sung to stony-faced statues were able to procure the end of the dictatorship and all its horrendous excesses.

Along the way, you lost your faith. So many young men cut down, so many families destroyed, despite the supplications, invocations, and ritual sacrifices. Jean-Édouard was detained and murdered, despite the protection of the Vodou spirits, despite the prayers of your mother, who insisted on taking you two to church bright and early on the day after the Vodou ritual. He was killed like so many others. Like my father, even if you never really talked about it. I know they took his life with no regard for him, his family, or friends, as if they were slaughtering a lowly chicken.

Before your death, you returned zealously to your childhood faith, just as a bird whose wings are exhausted desperately sets down somewhere. The Lord's ways are inscrutable, you used to tell me. And you asked me to have a requiem sung for you in the Descailles parish church and to bury you in the family vault, next to Jean-Édouard.

How could I forgo this final gesture of tenderness and loyalty, or fail to honor this request murmured in your failing but proud voice? Without regard to the extravagant cost, I took the airplane to your island with the bitter memory of my temporary estrangement from you. In my attempt to erase all your stories from my memory, I had spurned you, refused your calls, distanced myself from you. I would love to have your faith and be able to salve my conscience by striking my breast a few times. But all I have is the irrefutable logic of my atheism—plus a heart racked with self-anger and, in spite of myself, with anger toward you.

Two years after earning my secondary school certificate, I practically severed our ties. It didn't take you long to notice. You had stayed in Fort-de-France, awaiting my calls. With the regularity of a chore, I used to telephone you every week. Our conversations were brief and invariably hurried, and I banished all mention of Quisqueya, its history, or its geography. I would refuse to acknowledge any allusion to its political situation, showing no reaction to the half-caustic, half-rueful humor you reserved for problems affecting your part of the island. The worst betrayal: I purged all Quisqueyan turns of phrase when speaking with you, even though I was familiar with the languages of both territories and would normally have passed effortlessly from Martinican Creole to the native language of your homeland. I could feel your disappointment over the phone line; it pervaded my silences and magnified my remorse. Still, those conversations were too much for me, Maman. I used to feel cornered, and hanging up was my only means of survival. But often this calculated aloofness would gnaw at me, leaving invisible wounds: around me floated the repugnant stench of a traitor without a country.

« »

The Deceased often showed flashes of genius. To be sure, other presidents before him had pushed their spouses to the forefront. As good and faithful representatives of their husbands, these first ladies, dressed in their Sunday finery and wearing elegant hats, often dedicated buildings. Madame Magritte, adorned in gold and pearls, had inaugurated the Fair of the Cosmos. Madame Vénérable hosted a whole series of receptions at the Port-du-Roi International Exposition. All of them distributed gifts to orphans and delivered speeches to federations of women's clubs, agricultural cooperatives, and adolescent mothers groups. "Adolescent mothers"—she despised that euphemism for unwed mothers, which took her back to her birth, to the shameful scar of being abandoned by both parents. How could someone be an adolescent and a mother at the same time? Simultaneously juvenile and responsible, adult and powerless?

She had vowed not to bring a child into the world without first having a ring on her finger. Vowed not to expose herself to that dishonor, not to sacrifice another human being to an egotistical craving for motherhood under inappropriate circumstances. But she would not have married just anyone. Fortunately, her caramel skin allowed her to be choosy, spared her from having to throw herself at the first man to come along, enabled her to give careful study to the field of eligible suitors—accountants, bailiffs, schoolteachers, and other professional men with no great future. From the very first, she had sensed the Deceased's limitless ambition, his compulsion to put forth the best of himself, to reshape unfavorable circumstances. Each person creates a destiny. She had perceived in him the capacity to influence hers. She hadn't been wrong.

« »

How long was that sterile break in our relationship? I re-entered your history so abruptly that it sometimes seems the interruption was minimal. With no transition. Wisely, you never mentioned that period to me. Instead, we settled into a modus vivendi consisting of thoughts left unsaid, of ever-present memories overlaid like transparent veils. As our relationship resumed, we gently touched this or that one to avoid disturbing them too much. I renewed my prior tendency toward muted shades of sadness.

When I received my cousin's distress call from Martinique, I took the next flight as if I were diving off a sinking ship: conscious of the danger to be confronted, yet having no alternative but to jump into the sea. Your illness, which became your last agony, thrust me into a desperate state that still tears me apart. A myriad of administrative hassles took up my time, without dislodging the stinging pain that seized me after your passing. The shipment of the body from Fort-de-France to Port-du-Roi, the arrogance of people unable to comprehend your wish to be buried in a country where life was in tatters. The flight across Quisqueya, the sight of those scraggly hills, then the journey to Descailles in an off-road vehicle that churned up clouds of whitish dust on the bumpy tracks. The occasional glimpses of the sparkling sea, and my absurd belief that the heady tang of the salt air was making you tipsy. The cousins' tearful welcome, their desperate sincerity that overcame their reflexive envy of my privileged situation, their unconsciously imploring looks, the yawning gap between their means and mine. All those things magnified my feelings of intense solitude as I attended to the various tasks without wanting to bid you farewell.

On my return to France, while I struggled to recover from my fatigue, the disturbing dreams began their nightly visitations. Soon afterward, as if to give substance to the macabre atmosphere that surrounded me, I first entered that woman's room and encountered the face that was so recognizable, despite the ravages inflicted by exile and old age. The face that today epitomizes for me all the horrors of a regime that left its grim mark on my native country.

« »

Among the Deceased's predecessors, several aspired to be known as builders: Loiseau, the Americans' puppet; Vénérable, no doubt acting in good faith, but hostage to his fears; and even that strutting military man, Pierre-Albert. All of them spread their names on the walls of housing projects: Cité Loiseau at La Fossette. Cité Duverneau Vénérable at Front de Mer, Cités Magritte I and II laid out one behind the other. Only the Deceased thought of constructing a development in honor of his wife, the first lady. Given the symbolism of the gesture, she wouldn't dwell on minor details: the misaligned streets, the disorganized layout of the buildings, the walls as flimsy as cardboard. Besides, they had quickly been able to conceal those unsightly structures behind rows of townhouses built to accommodate a good number of the party faithful. Thus, they killed two birds with one stone: they satisfied the natural human longing for a permanent place to live, and they rewarded many of their most devoted followers. A stroke of genius by the Deceased. And a memorable gesture with respect to his wife. She was deeply satisfied to have a community named after her. Rewarded a hundred times over for the anguish she suffered from the attempted coups, the live bombs that failed to explode, the invasions in the four corners of the country. To experience her day of glory at last was well worth all the upheaval.

« »

The first time I set eyes on the old woman, I truly believed that those nightmares of yours had become mine and were pursuing me in broad daylight, unfolding right before my eyes, bringing to life the principal characters of your horrific soap operas. Despite her shrunken and almost cadaverous form, I immediately recognized—with all due respect to the nursing home director—the pinched lips and aristocratic cheekbones. The newsreels and photos had accurately captured the enigmatic upturn of her lips, so distant that it didn't qualify as a smile. I automatically thought of one of your innumerable stories.

You always spoke of her in a disdainful and sarcastic tone, like the time you described her playing the role of grande dame at the dedication of the Cité Odile Savien Doréval. For an entire week, the ceremony was shown repeatedly on state television, and the newspapers gave the story front-page coverage. The public heard about nothing else. She bestowed her name on a neighborhood where inhuman deprivation planted itself with its legs wide apart and its buttocks exposed to the wind. Gave her name like a slap to the hopelessness of those people who struggled to survive with no potable water, no latrines, in hovels that grew like weeds on a muddy patch of ground. Who were offered neither guidance nor respect. Shamefully, she took unconcealed pride in showing off her long-sleeved silk dress and a chapeau she could have worn in a stage play. First lady: a euphemism for dolled-up decadence.

« »

More distinguished than ever, and with her hair gathered atop her head to accent the delicacy of her profile and the elegance of her neck, she stepped into the official limousine that was to take her to the new housing project. Cité Odile Savien Doréval. She was wearing a new dress, of course, whipped up by that mulatto woman whose name she could no longer recall. The one she would ask the Deceased to summon in the middle of the night to take their daughters' measurements and to bring her catalog for them to look at. In the midst of the nightly curfews and blackouts, while rumors poisoned their existence to the point that the Doréval children, incapable of sleeping, would whine, sulk, or quarrel among themselves. The fashion designer, who was on the palace payroll, would show up incognito in an official car and unpack her fabrics and ribbons, a world of shimmering fantasy. She would produce her tape measure and her fashion magazines. The girls used to gather around her, their eyes gleaming. For a few hours, they seemed to forget their gilded prison. Sometimes, from the height of one of the terraces, the Deceased would watch, impassively, yet she knew he was touched by the sight of their enjoyment. Just as it touched her to see them marvel at the swatches of silk, net, or muslin, and wrangle over who would have the prettiest fabric or the most beautiful design. Meanwhile, beyond the palace, conspiracies were taking shape, and opponents were swarming in all directions, creating an oppressive atmosphere that reached even the Dorévals' home and hearth.

For the dedication ceremony, she had chosen a silky fabric, with the kind of geometric shapes she loved, varying in hue from green to yellow. She selected a style she judged to be discreet yet elegant, with long sleeves befitting an occasion of this importance and a straight neckline with pearl buttons on the bodice. The cut underscored the refinement of her neck and posture. As for jewelry, she wore only her customary rings, the ones that could be seen glittering in the photos. She had opted for one of her latest wigs, styled quite modishly. Fabien had found her to his liking when she had joined him in their private parlor, and he had favored her with a more lingering look than usual. A promising omen.

All through the ceremony, in which she had received floral bouquets from the children of the new development, her emotion never waned. And to think that in 1987 the authorities had rechristened the area "Cité Ochan,"* after Radio Ochan,* the station that had instigated a collective protest movement against their regime, hiding behind falsely religious and cultural messages. In any case, nothing could wipe away her satisfaction.

Besides, it's lucky that the neighborhood no longer bears her name, now that it has become so squalid and hideous that the international media display its image as an iconic symbol of Quisqueya's poverty and violence.

« »

Now and then, to lighten the atmosphere, I would encourage you to recount less bitter, less bloody stories, including the irresistible anecdotes about the dictator's blunders. The affair of the fake Arab sheik, a self-declared Yemeni, persisted as one of your favorites and always brought an unabashed smile to your lips.

The subject of your deceased brother was almost invariably poignant, but I knew how to coax you into describing the brighter moments, the amusing or endearing episodes of Jean-Édouard's short life. Your nights out as a group, the weekend flirtations, the madcap adventures. Such as the time your brother, then aged twelve, climbed up on the roof of the house with your two cousins. Armed with an old mirror, they regaled themselves by sending blinding reflections toward the house of Mademoiselle Virginie Cadet, a friend of the family, an old maid with a peevish disposition, always quick to report the mischievous doings of the neighborhood children to their parents. So, when the boys discovered that they could send dazzling beams of light through Mademoiselle Virginie's windows, they had a field day. Naturally, it didn't take very long for the old spinster to identify the source of the intrusive and unwelcome reflections, and that very evening she came to lodge a complaint.

Jean-Édouard and the cousins received an epic thrashing, but took their revenge at the start of the next school year. They sent Mademoiselle Virginie a passionate love letter, signed in the name of her next-door neighbor, a physician and widower who was still good-looking but rather befuddled. Soon afterward Mademoiselle Virginie came to tell your mother the story with uncharacteristically effusive expressions and gestures. As if by chance, she was decked out as never before in garish makeup. Concealed behind a door, Jean-Édouard overheard how she interpreted the physician's missive, which according to her revealed a brilliant mind, a touching sensitivity, and an exemplary delicacy. "He never looked at me inappropriately, never spoke to me impertinently. Instead, he was conducting a discreet courtship. What maturity! What culture!" "What bunk, you mean!" mocked Jean-Édouard, who for a few gourdes had hired an older student to compose the letter on an unlined sheet. I adored that story, which revealed to me a fun-loving uncle, a mischievous and companionable prankster, reinforcing my sense of loss at never having known him, yet bringing to my heart a lightness that bore an odd resemblance to happiness.

Sadly, the amusing stories constituted only a meager proportion of your repertoire, and the ghastly accounts soon regained their predominance. The story of the Rally for Friendship, to which Jean-Édouard had briefly belonged prior to his death, followed directly after that of Mademoiselle Virginie. Under the direction of the Spiritan priests, young men and women took part in various activities, such as choral music, reading clubs, and discussion groups. To escape, however briefly, the claws of repression. They exchanged views, sang together, fell in love, questioned the Church as "intelligent Catholics encouraged to pursue a spirit of inquiry"—within the limits of the faith, of course. Sorting through your possessions at Fort-de-France, I found a dog-eared but clean copy of *I've Lost the Faith,* by Henri Engelmann. You often cited this work, which was the subject of debates within the Rally. The ideals of liberty and free expression often sparked a tumultuous clash between the convictions of the priests and those of the young people drawn to a Marxist ideology. And yet, the need to resist and stand up to repression bonded the group more than faith or dogma.

The young man who would become my father had also belonged to this group. Years later, he, too, was to be cravenly slain during the regime of Jean-Paul Doréval. For that matter, hadn't every one of the dictatorship's murders been contemptible? I was familiar with so many horrendous stories of disappearances, arrests, and tortures that, at the risk of sounding irreverent, my father's gruesome fate seemed to me just one of many.

Your mother had misgivings about the Rally. She did not want Jean-Édouard to attend its meetings. With all the certitude of the mother of a humble family, she saw that disaster would strike sooner or later and that it was better not to stand in its path. "Why bring down the dictator's thunderbolt on your head? Why risk your life at those choir rehearsals and film clubs? The priests would hide behind their cassocks, and you young people would be the first victims." She sensed the impending catastrophe. She knew, however, that you can't stop a gale by holding up your hand. Her maternal anguish, stronger than her rational side and more integral than her past as a militant feminist under Vénérable, brought to her lips the warnings she secretly expected your brother to ignore.

«»

After the Deceased's electoral victory, she had often imagined her public appearances as first lady, but the very first ovation set off dazzling sparkles of light. She wasn't expecting the intense sensuous pleasure. An ecstatic feeling spread through her limbs, leaving her quivering with delight. She was finally at the place that was rightfully hers. She would be able to act as she had wanted for so long. She was surprised at first by the ease with which she was adopting this role, fulfilling the functions of a first lady, officiating at the Deceased's side without ever falling short.

Even at the most difficult moments. The invasion attempts, the revolts, the acts of defiance, the bombs, the rumors—it was those, in particular, that furrowed her brow with concern. Every morning, hearing—or pretending not to hear—what machinations were afoot, who was daring to threaten their peace of mind, what lies were spewing from the clandestine Radio Hirondelle and setting conversations abuzz from one household to another. Cracks in the social order that she had to hide from the Deceased and the children, so they would not widen into raging streams and carry away her dignity and courage. She regularly gathered up her pride, like a warrior girding his loins to face an enemy. Never any regrets, never so much as a side step that could be viewed as a retreat. Rumors of fateful dates, of deadlines and ultimatums, passed through the palace walls and sometimes upset the children terribly.

She had always endeavored to maintain her elegance and distinction, even on that summer's day very early in their reign

when the Deceased asked her to pack their luggage. When the
imminent danger of defeat threw them into a helter-skelter of
jostling and scrambling. Shoes, hats, compromising documents.
The uncertain situation outside. The threats. The urgent calls
to the foreign embassies, the relief afforded by the Colombian
embassy's response. The wait, the insidious fear, always ready
to infiltrate the space between words, the depths of a silence.
The rebels had occupied the Desravines barracks. What an outrage! They threatened to attack unless the president abdicated.
Had he been ousted, his term would have lasted less than a year.
Fortunately, the rebels didn't understand the magnitude of the
task they had undertaken.

All around Fabien and her, so many evil-intentioned people, caring only for their self-interest and capable of double-
crossing him at any moment. The Deceased never placed total
confidence in anyone. Who could blame him for that? Almost
all the attempted overthrows, the invasions, the botched coups,
the attacks, and the bombings came from people who were
close to him, including former colleagues and military men
connected to the regime. Of course, the enemies didn't just sit
around, either. Wasn't it the former supporters of Magritte who
fomented the action that was carried out with such amateur-
ism and lack of discipline? Did the insurgents take the trouble
to conduct reconnaissance before launching their operation?
Some months before, the Deceased had stored arms and muni-
tions at the palace, precisely in anticipation of a possible attempted rebellion.

The most inconceivable part of the affair is that the three
individuals who dared to attack the supreme head of the nation —she didn't count the foreigners implicated in the affair—
allowed themselves to be undone by the stupid matter of a cigarette. One of them sent Julio, the same Julio who served as
the first lady's chauffeur, to buy cigarettes! Julio was quickly
forced to reveal how few conspirators there really were. Incapable of controlling their nicotine habit, and yet they wanted to
snatch power. Has anyone ever seen such military officers and ex-
officers? No matter. Soldiers never lose their bravado. Stupid to

the point of conducting no surveillance before setting off such alarm in the country. Deluding themselves that, despite all their carelessness, they could lead the Quisqueyan people.

In this instance, the Deceased decided to teach other potential troublemakers a lesson. Moreover, the people spontaneously took matters into their own hands and slashed the traitors' bodies with machetes. Dragged one of them all the way to the palace. That was the day the Deceased put on his officer's cap, brandished his rifle, and showed his followers that he was right with them, leading the struggle.

She used to liken the Deceased's resolve to that of the bourgeoisie hell-bent on clinging to its privileges, regardless of the era or the regime in power. She had observed from afar the affluence of the vested interests, accustomed for so long to full possession of the land, material resources, and power. Before she became used to it herself! Some of them would never forgive the Deceased for breaking their iron grip on the apparatus of the state, for having curbed their stranglehold on commerce and the economy. Out of all the disloyal schemes that had burdened their existence during the fourteen years of the regime in its first iteration—the authentic one—a sizeable proportion came from hostile segments of the bourgeoisie and the Catholic Church. Both factions were always ready to unite against the national interest if they weren't kept in check.

The Deceased understood this perfectly. In October 1966 he appointed native-born members of the clergy to lead the Church in Quisqueya. This was the only solution that would ensure the sincere and loyal collaboration of the Church in favor of the Quisqueyan people, who were then battling the agony of famine. The first Quisqueyan archbishop of Port-du-Roi and four indigenous bishops at last! To guide the people in their quest for spirituality. Pope Paul VI did not make the mistake of objecting. In the presence of the first lady and a group of children, the papal emissary gave the Deceased medals depicting Christ and the Fathers of the Church. His Holiness likewise sent his photo inscribed with his most ardent wishes for the religious welfare of the Quisqueyan people and a thriving Christianity *among them. What a lesson for the detractors who tried to capitalize on the conflicts between a few malevolent foreign churchmen and the revolutionary regime! When the Deceased received the new Quisqueyan prelates at the palace, national pride blossomed forth everywhere. Manual laborers, functionaries, salesclerks, peddlers, even the field hands understood the importance of these appointments! She almost smiled when she thought of the slightly overenthusiastic words of one of the new bishops: "Your Excellency, you have proclaimed a new independence!"*

At the same time, the Deceased would never have repudiated Vodou the way some of his predecessors had. Every weapon at hand must be put to use. Both Catholicism and Vodouism had their place. It was a matter of knowing how to manipulate faith and religious practice. The success of the Dorévalist regime lay precisely in its melding of different creeds. Culminating in its own glorification! To have an adjective derived from their name! To have treatises written about their years in power. She had read and reread them during this exile that she had not expected, despite the countless warning signs that had heralded the end of the Heir's regime. Why should she have paid more attention to them than to all the sensational rumors that had enlivened the Deceased's fourteen-year reign? Even as the ougans* *they consulted were assuring them that the revolution would endure, witness accounts told of the resentment of other* ougans *who were forced to pay fees to conduct their rituals. Naturally, every segment of society had to contribute toward the work of national rehabilitation, but certain unscrupulous types were exploiting the power the Deceased had conferred on them and using it to enrich themselves. That's why the Deceased administered severe punishments at times. The revolution sometimes chastised its own children. If they failed to understand its importance and stained it with their insatiable greed, they deserved no mercy.*

She shifted a little in her bed, feeling against her skin the roughness of the cotton sheet that had been washed too many times. Try as she might, her weary mind could not conjure up the silky feeling of her undergarments of bygone days and the freshness of the delicately perfumed bed linens. She imagined herself instead in the dormitory amid the disagreeable odors of the orphanage, and she fought against the sense of defeat that was stalking her.

«»

You never stopped telling me about your parents, especially your mother. That strong and valiant woman who, like so many others in the early days, had enthusiastically embraced the speeches of Fabien Doréval. Disgusted with the discriminatory practices of the governments of Loiseau and Stivio Valais, she had aligned herself with Doréval's promises of justice and equality, of social and economic inclusion for individuals cast aside because of their color, class, or rural origins. She soon became disillusioned. The daughter of peasants transplanted to Port-au-Roi, a schoolteacher by profession, she had thought that the ardent campaigner against tuberculosis in the countryside would work to improve the lot of the landless poor. Alas! Papa Fab didn't clean up much in our social system. Stories of farmers conscripted to attend stage-managed rallies were soon followed by tales of peasants forcibly displaced from their land.

You often told me the story of Fasilia, a rice vendor whose clientele included your mother. This woman had lost her son, a tall, strapping lad with muscles hardened by twenty-two years of toiling in the rice fields. During a lull in business, she came over to you and your mother and shared her troubles. These had started with the extortion carried out by Papa Fab's regional administrators and the theft of *carreaux de terre** inherited from a great-grandfather. A story as old and unjust as that of the land redistribution following Quisqueya's independence in 1804, a process in which the peasants came out, as always, on the losing end. The family had clung to those scraps of land even when Uncle Joseph decided to leave for Cuba, even when little cousin Jezila fell gravely ill. Acreage preserved at the price of unimaginable sacrifices, the sale of the last ox and two pigs, mouths even thirstier than before, torsos even scrawnier amid their destitution. Then a bulky gentleman from the city came through their gate with the regional boss behind him. They es-

62 MEMORY AT BAY

corted the father to a spot beneath a spreading mango tree and spoke to him at length. The two visitors were wearing the famous dark glasses, but in any event no one dared to look them in the eyes. Mustn't stare at the devil. The father signed, of course. Otherwise, the men would have taken him away, along with all the other males of the family: the son, the nephews, the cousins. He was given a pittance, a few hundred gourdes for more than ten acres of land. The father dropped dead a month later—thankfully for him, as he would not have survived what happened next. The blue-suited predators returned later in the season and carted off several local peasants. At the time, Fasilia was away fetching water from the spring with her youngest daughter. The men forced her son Gabriel and his cousins to climb aboard a truck; it was May 22, 1962.

You told me with your ironic smile that May 22 was a memorable date for all Quisqueyans, but especially for the peasants. Even illiterates have it inscribed in their memories in purple hues, like the tall flowers at funerals: National Independence Day. Fasilia kept repeating that phrase, spitting on the ground each time. On that hallowed day, she returned from the well to find her remaining family members wailing. She journeyed to the capital, inquired at the police stations, and roamed the hospital corridors, the forbidding precincts of the morgue, and the prison waiting rooms, all without finding her son. To maintain her illusion of being close to Gaby, she stayed in Port-du-Roi, selling rice, her only link with the lost rice fields on the banks of the Lenglesou. Each time she brought you her produce, she would retell her story in the futile hope of easing her pain, which only mounted in the same measure as her voice and gestures. She would mourn her son's vigorous blood, his arms the color of ripe eggplants, his laugh stronger than the hard work of cultivation. And she would always end with this plaintive and indignant question: "What have they done to my son?"

Sometimes your mother would fidget nervously as she listened to Fasilia. She would have liked to tell her to be quiet, to be careful, not to broadcast her story to all and sundry, for she risked getting herself dragged off, as well. Her tale resembled so many other narratives of stolen lands, vanished sons, sorrows buried with the dead. But your mother also knew, Maman, that each affliction creates its own laws and that to annul or change them requires shedding so many tears and so much blood that they are often immutable.

I also knew by heart how the story ended. Fasilia converted her rice stall into a business selling household goods, plastic plates, and bowls of every color, bogging down in her marginal existence in Port-au-Roi and separating more and more from her former life on the riverbank. With another woman from her village whom she met by chance, she found lodging in the environs of the Vallières market. She never found her son. Run over by a car that didn't even stop, she died at Port-du-Roi's main public hospital. A banal enough story. After all, how could the death of a displaced, impoverished, and miserable peasant make any difference?

Your mother's prediction of the Spiritan priests' survival came true, but under a different scenario. Despite their clerical garb, they were unceremoniously expelled.

You always reminded me that the fifteenth of August was a holiday in your country. The feast of Our Lady of the Assumption. Our Lady of Perpetual Help, Patroness of Quisqueya. Did your patroness reveal a sense of irony in letting you stagnate in a state of perpetual calamity, in contrast to her promise that if you pray to her faithfully, she will be equally loyal in aiding you? Port-du-Roi learned the news quickly, because it always arrives somewhere, slips under the doors, shakes the sleepers, and electrifies peacefully slumbering brains. Thus would arrive rumors of coups d'état that made hope expand, only to deflate afterward, like a balloon forlornly fizzling. The bad news, arrests, indiscriminate shootings, and executions were met with resignation, despondency, anger, resentment, or most commonly, with sighs that blended all of those emotions. A neighbor came to report that the regime had ousted about fifteen priests from the elite school where they taught and ordered their deportation. On hearing this, your mother instinctively crossed herself. Then she went out to investigate after ordering you not to budge.

Since you weren't permitted to go out alone in any case,

"don't budge" meant literally to stay seated and wait for her and particularly not to venture out on the veranda. Since Jean-Édouard's death, you had become the focus of your mother's anxieties. Your father was gradually killing himself with small doses of rum and cigarettes. Was he aware of your presence, or did he think that, like your brother, you no longer existed? I know that his passivity hurt you. He shut himself up in his anguish, while leaving you all alone to find a way of handling your own pain. In contrast, your mother clung to you to avoid total collapse and surrounded you with prohibitions.

She returned in less than an hour, staggered by the reliable news, elicited from a neighbor whose sister worked in the sacristy of the Port-du-Roi cathedral. The sister had heard it directly from the rector. The expulsion order involved nine priests and a lay brother. Your mother reeled off their names. You told me two of them: Albert Andral and Passy Preux. Your big brother had spoken of them; he often conversed with them, sometimes holding stormy discussions about the duty of religion to address the country's predicament, paths of resistance, and the decisive battle to be waged. Against whom? Against what? Ultimately, Jean-Édouard had left the Rally several months before his death, while staying in touch with several of his comrades. You had never met those priests, but on hearing their names on the list of deportees, it seemed to you that your big brother was dying all over again. You began to tremble. Your mother understood when she heard your arms strike the table convulsively. She sat down heavily without a word.

《 》

While the memories of the past ten years were blurring into the malaise of her exile and hardly mattered to her, far more distant scenes were nonetheless sharply emerging. At the lightest vibration of her thoughts, particular images were taking shape. They were the ones that made her most fearful because they were suffused with flesh and blood.

On bad days, Fabien would tirelessly repeat the names of all those he needed to eliminate. As if to dare his listeners to instigate a plot of some kind. The names rolled on, with no need to evoke at much length the circumstances attached to each: they all pertained to former friendships. A wife with whom she had discussed hairstyles and fashion, youngsters who had played with the Doréval children. Sometimes they would learn that the father of a child to whom they had just given a birthday present had taken refuge in a Latin American embassy. Had received a fusillade in the back while trying to escape arrest. Had perished along with his entire family during an abortive uprising in the course of which the VSN had again proved worthy of the president's confidence. Over the years she had learned not to recall the sweet little faces, to close her mind's eye so as not to visualize the expression of terror on a known face. She had put on the impenetrable mask of the photos and official ceremonies. Over the years it had become so easy. As usual, she wanted to banish all nagging qualms and retain only the thoughts that would facilitate her journey back in time, but she could only manage to take the whole bundle of memories with her into an unquiet sleep.

« »

August 15, 1969. So many dates stained with blood and tears. The pages of the calendar commemorate so many dead. And yet, I sometimes have the impression that all the victims' names have simply been erased and the dates emptied of their significance, as lifeless as corpses.

You told me that on August 15, 1969, you were sure that life was ending. You were not yet sixteen, Maman. There was no prospect of your going to visit your friend, Magali, the younger sister of Rony, a member of the Rally for Friendship chorale. No question of going out. Besides, where would you have gone? The government had issued a decree banning all meetings. No more gatherings of young men under utility poles, where they would watch the girls go by and speak of life in flurries of racy jokes and pop songs. No more rest breaks in the shade of a tree for workers to revive their courage and grit before confronting their families and the duties that awaited them. No more whispered parleys outside the church, where gossipers would meet to exchange the latest rumors. Abolished: the convivial afternoon discussions about the tedium of days without work and the dispiritingly quiet nights. Forbidden: life.

During the week following the priests' expulsions, your mother barred you from leaving the house. Even the veranda was off-limits. You were forbidden to sit out there and watch the neighborhood residents pass, to return their greetings, or to listen to the merriment of children still too innocent to gauge the size of the cloud over their future. I imagine your days shut up in the study, with books as your only companions. I know how much you adored reading, but what torment it must have been for you to endure this isolation without other young voices to keep you sane! No one to share your turmoil and your anxieties. No question of talking in front of—much less with—the servants about the events that were making hearts beat fast. Your mother also discouraged visits and brusquely sent away Jean-Édouard's friends, who were seeking the comfort of a friendly encounter. The dictatorship was insidiously eating away at Grand-mère's humanity.

I slowly approach the form stretched out on the bed. It seems to me that the old woman has made an unusual noise, not one of those indistinct groans that elderly or seriously ill people emit in their sleep, but something closer to a wakeful state, something more conscious. I move toward her like a sleepwalker, as if gradually emerging from my musings. The bony fingers grasp the sheet firmly, while the impassive expression, closed eyes, and frail, debilitated body suggest lethargy and fragility. I stay watching the invalid for a long time, scanning her features for any glimmer of intelligence and life, a sign other than the irregular breathing that gently lifts the sheet. For a long time, I listen to the old woman's silence. Sense the tug of her gravitational field. Then I deliberately enter it.

THREE

THE WIFE AND THE ORPHAN

While still very young, I became an expert at choosing inoffensive subjects, ones that wouldn't provoke a long diatribe from you against the Doréval dictatorships or those rare silences that were the precursors of your days of utter prostration. But today I wonder whether my ploy accomplished much at all. Whether you, Maman, didn't carry an inexpressible sadness with you to your grave. And whether I who vicariously experienced the despotic regime won't always have it under my skin. I've heard so much about those people since my childhood—not only the Doréval family, but also the notorious henchmen with their revealing or deceptive nicknames, still evocative of terrible anecdotes long after their time: Ti Baba, Captain Henry Tobias, Evaris Maître, Chief Lanfè, Lucien Désir, Colonel Britton Claudius. They've become elements of my universe, so powerful a part of my mental space and of my memories that it seems to me I'll never be able to escape them and will always remain captive to their ghosts.

« »

Her own silence practically smothered her. She made a concerted effort to escape from the void, to retrieve the thread of her thoughts, not to lose her grip. Not yet. So many things to untangle for her personal benefit. Hers alone, for once. She mustn't think any more about the young woman whose persistence in scrutinizing her never faltered. Rarely did any animation show on the young woman's fine, yet somber, face, and then just fleetingly, like a twitch. The absurd thought came to Odile that she and the caregiver were playing hide-and-seek without knowing or wanting to. Mutually hiding their faces so as not to be seen. She struggled against her impulse to approach the young woman's dense melancholy, touch it with her finger, and wrap herself in it, too. She tried hard to purge everything from her mind. To stop thinking about the children, the Deceased, and everyone else. She no longer wanted to be a mere adjunct, the part of the couple that always followed the "and," as if she couldn't exist independently. As if her own story had no importance in the larger scheme.

She didn't regret anything. Blubbering and remorse were alien to her character, but she could now look at her married life in a new way. Without worrying about her failure to behave as a good wife. She admitted to herself that she had drawn considerable comfort from the stability of the marriage and the family, in spite of her fierce need for independence. The difficult beginnings, the modest lodgings in the Rue de l'Enterrement, her lonely year during Fabien's overseas study in Missouri, the uncertainty regarding his absence, the anxiety for the future— none of that detracted in the slightest from the sense of well-being that a home set on firm foundations brought her, if only because she was confident of Fabien's love. She, the abandoned orphan, flourished in the solidity and routine of everyday life.

But nearly sixteen years after their marriage, when the Deceased leapt into the political fray, she, too, threw herself into it, wholeheartedly. She understood then that a part of her was waiting to reveal itself fully in that environment of struggle, ambition, clashing ideas, betrayals, and dubious alliances. Understood, also, that she had spent long enough keeping up their pathetic lodgings and working in health centers frequented by derelicts whose lives were doomed at the outset. She moved into the National Palace without apprehensions, but with the firm intention of staying there as long as possible. She congratulated herself on having chosen a husband so successfully.

« »

The wedding of Jean-Paul Doréval and Isabelle Baudet took place several months before our departure for Martinique. From its inception, that year had proved remarkable for our family. As if once again familial events coincided with occurrences that were convulsing the life of the nation. First of all, the loss of both your parents within a two-month span. You told me that after your marriage your parents had begun slowly withdrawing from you. My birth brought them a measure of happiness, but their contentment was almost ethereal, already detached from the world. They'd decided it was time for them to rejoin Jean-Édouard. They didn't say this in so many words, but you heard your mother mumble that their old bones were clamoring for rest (though neither of them was yet sixty-five!), that they'd had enough of this world. While feeling abandoned, you couldn't blame them for wanting to escape their ordeal. For how do parents carry on after the death of their child? After the loss of a son in such circumstances? How do they summon the will to get out of bed after restless nights spent imagining the suffering and torment of a being they would have wanted to protect from the tiniest scratch?

Sometimes a sadly complicit smile would pass between them, and you would feel excluded, already deprived of their presence. They used to lavish attention on me, their only grandchild, so avid were they to draw some small consolation from the spontaneous and light-hearted affection of a child. From time to time, with gentle caresses of your arm, a firmer pressure of their lips on your forehead, glances that were misty-eyed yet determined, they were saying good-bye to you. When your father, the first to go, died of a heart attack, you knew that your mother would soon follow. And in fact, you were just starting to recover from the first bereavement when an attack of hypertension carried away Grand-mère. Two funerals in less than three months. I don't recall much of that period, although you told me many times that in the beginning I kept asking for my grandparents. Still, childhood shielded me from the more devastating aspects of grief.

Once in Fort-de-France, however, you tried hard to rekindle my family memories. It was a tradition of ours to visit your maternal grandparents during the summer break. They had settled in Descailles in the house you called the house of flowers because your grandmother had planted oleanders, daisies, and hibiscus bushes all around. Your mother had always wanted to return to the city of her birth to live out her days. Even though they'd grown up in Port-du-Roi, both she and your father came from the South, that region of hills and plains, of shifting terrain. The nearby ocean was like an immense blue veil, tingeing the atmosphere and the ever-present ranges of hills. A low-lying city, Descailles fell prey to hurricanes even before it became the practice to name them. Nowadays bearing disarmingly familiar names like Flora and Allen, their menace still weighs annually on the city.

In fact, a particularly dangerous storm season was responsible for your presence in the capital on that fateful August fifteenth. Normally, you would have been in Descailles celebrating the feast of Our Lady of the Assumption.

When you were little, your grandmother Eugénie, known to you as Man Nini, would stand outside her cottage waiting for you and Jean-Édouard. A battered old bus would drop you, your brother, and your mother there. Through the bus window, you told me, you could see Man Nini standing with open arms. As if she had spent the entire year waiting in front of her door for her loved ones. The next day she would lead you and Jean-Édouard far out of town into the cornfields.

Even with your persistent prompting, however, I couldn't remember the annual visits that you, Papa, and I made to Man Nini after your parents died. Before we left for Fort-de-France. While Papa was alive.

I would be very glad if those cheery remembrances came back to me. For the time being, I can only borrow yours. I imagine you as a little girl astride a donkey, deathly afraid on the bumpy trail, your arms clutching the animal's neck and your eyes shining with nervous excitement. You would not have exchanged your place for anything in the world. The vacations with Man Nini were timeless days of sanctuary from the infamous years of tyranny, a small enclave of childhood bliss for you to savor. While you were telling me about it, you became carefree again, lively and sparkling.

Of course, as the dictatorship grew more severe, it became harder and harder for you to get to Descailles for your summer vacations. Your mother was hesitant to venture out on the roads with you and your brother. At the time, it was dangerous to travel from one region to another. Traveling to Descailles had always entailed fording rivers and streams. Sometimes your party would spend the night on the riverbank and set off again in the morning when the waters became passable. Now there was the added risk of coming upon Tonton Macoutes greedy for the money they could extort from the bus passengers or simply intent on flaunting their power. Consequently, the trip lost much of its appeal. And yet, when you arrived at Man Nini's, you would immediately forget the immense but agreeable fatigue that had set you dozing on the bus, you'd forget the fear and the tedium. You would see only the prospect of a sojourn between sun and sea and of evenings passed under a crystalline sky alive with stars.

How happy I was to hear you enliven your recollections in that way, to discover several oases of joy, playful and welcoming spaces that offset the usual gloomy mists. I adopted the phrase "the days of sweet memory" to describe those moments when, your eyes pensive and luminous, you would share your morsels of happiness. On those days you would also recount your everyday activities in Port-du-Roi: your fits of helpless laughter, the sudden acrobatic stunts that startled your mother, those peaceful interludes in which you were lost in the universe of a book, the innocent squabbles that sometimes led to parental swats and tearful outbursts. Under the watchful eyes of parents who were protecting you from everything, not just the threat of VSN militiamen. In those days, you insisted, the adults contented themselves with being parents. They didn't aspire to become their children's friends at all costs and to confide in them about everything; and so they spared them a great many worries. Only as an adult did you learn that some evenings you had almost gone hungry for want of money, that the store where your mother relied on credit to buy the fabric for your school uniforms was demanding payment by month's end, that school tuition charges had gone up again. In those days, before terrifying tales of the Tonton Macoutes came to dominate everyone's imagination, children would go to sleep with only the anxiety of an uncompleted homework assignment or their dismay over the scary story heard before bedtime.

Indeed, on the curfew evenings you children eagerly huddled together to hear blood-chilling yarns from the storyteller of the moment, whether it was the cook or your mother's elderly aunt who lived out her days in your household. From the veranda, you kids could catch the whispers of your parents and the closest neighbors, their heads drawn together to share the latest rumors. But what truly captivated the little ones was the tale that poured from the lips of the evening's storyteller. More fearful than the others, you nonetheless hung on her words, instantly forgetting your startled reactions to a chair scraping the floor or leaves rustling in a tree. Ignoring also the multiple warnings from your brother and cousins, who invariably dreamed up pranks to heighten your fear.

During the night the sharp crack of the *rara** band's leather whip threw you into such terror that you desperately wanted to cower in your parents' bedroom. Except that you would have had to go down the narrow corridor past a window overlooking a bleak little courtyard, where—according to your cousins—unimaginable events took place nightly. You learned much later that the boys who made fun of you and terrorized you by day hid their eyes at night and cringed in fear.

Trembling, bathed in sweat beneath your sheet, you would replay in your mind the stories you had heard. The ones about winged creatures with supernatural powers, about a little boy cured through the intervention of an aunt who'd been dead for five years, and about the sudden and mysterious death, exactly as foretold, of a colonel who'd made a pact with the devil. But in the morning, like a sun-kissed miracle, all your fears melted away with the first rays. During those summer days, with Jean-Édouard and the cousins who spent practically every summer at your place, you all frolicked in the courtyard. The boys were always less inhibited than you; as the only girl in the group, and also the youngest, you were saddled with a long list of dos and don'ts. Forbidden to climb trees, to talk boisterously with the neighbors, to go beyond the fence, to sit with your legs apart.

You used to smile tenderly at those memories before the wave of desolation came to claim you again.

« »

Her chest subsided farther under the weight of an inaudible sigh. Feeling more than seeing the circumspect gaze of the young aide turn toward her, she quickly recast her features to those of a decrepit old lady with lifeless eyes. Despite the surrounding silence and calm, a troubled feeling enveloped her. Oh! She wasn't mistaken about the physician's emotionless expression or about the brisk and sometimes curt manners of the head nurse. She also knew that death would not be too long in coming. People don't live forever. But the danger that was stalking her just then came from elsewhere; it was floating around her. Present, imminent. After a while, feeling tired and breaking off her effort to understand, she let her eyelids close.

« »

Nevertheless, I have met survivors of that era who had succeeded in putting the horror behind them, who had constructed a present without that pain like fresh blood ready to spurt, the pain you could never escape. With an expression you hoped would look serene, you used to mention various Quisqueyans, descendants of families victimized during the repression, who had changed their last names. First of all, to escape further violence, then to free themselves from the burden of the memories that clung to the familiar appellation. All mention of the name became a source of heartache and despair, of anger or remorse. For that reason, they had to adopt a new name that would not be associated with the regime's opponents, its accomplices, or even its innocent victims. This could be a demanding task, for in many families either an executioner or a victim could be identified, and sometimes both. Monsters and heroes, the fiendish and the honorable, sometimes found themselves united by the shared syllables.

The sense of guilt that overwhelms the survivors of a tragedy is sometimes occasioned by the sheer joy of seeing the sun

rise on a morning in the month of May. I learned very early
to recognize the guilt in your eyes: it would spring up without
warning, but most often after joys that were too full. In the next
moment your smile would contort with self-reproach, darken-
ing our happy times.

« »

*A glance can reveal a thought more clearly than a word. Ever
since childhood, she had mastered her own expression to the
point of giving it a detached and mysterious character, lightly
ironic, inoffensive without being vacuous. The first time she
set eyes on Fabien, a tremor ran through her. He didn't realize it—that's how skilled she was at controlling her body—but
she smelled the man's power just as you recognize the scent
of your native soil. Toughness and burning ambition beneath
a seemingly nondescript appearance. A nursing colleague had
told her one day, "It's easy to forget him if you've never met
his gaze, but once his eyes have rested on you, the mark of
Fabien Doréval doesn't leave you." She knew that behind her
back several nurses called her husband's look "the mark of the
beast." Did they really know him, those nurses who said they'd
crossed paths with him at the time of the anti-TB campaign?
Did they base their judgments on their first impressions or on
Fabien's subsequent actions? Whenever someone told a story
about the Deceased, it took on a particular coloration tied to
his rise to power.*

*His rise to power! She bristled at this hurtful expression, as if
Fabien was like all the others who had occupied the presidency,
every one of them addicted to power and its manifestations.
Without any real agenda. A year or two sufficed for them, as if
the mere fact of being installed in the seat of power, however
briefly, exhausted their ambitions. How demeaning to pass into
the history books that way, on the roster of presidents whose
hold on power had lasted two years or less! Fabien swore he
would not add his name to that lineage, regardless of predic-
tions to the contrary. Besides, their reign lasted much longer
than Fabien's fourteen years plus the fifteen years of Jean-Paul:
it was an entirely different mode of behavior, an attempt to re-*

trieve a sense of history, to rebuild the national sovereignty, to restore the people's dignity.

She realized that it was becoming more and more of a strain for her to think about all that, but she focused single-mindedly on her snatches of memory. All she had left was the luxury of dipping into the past, seeing and reliving it before letting go.

Her youth. A young girl with a proud step, anxious to avoid attracting just anyone, intent on telling the losers clearly and pointedly that they should give up. Nor was she interested in collecting bright-eyed, handsome young men who dreamed of entering the bourgeoisie, and she was never infatuated to the point of forgetting what was uppermost for them: a downtown department store, a factory in a working-class district, a thriving import business. At the orphanage, she had heard enough about certain patronesses—forthcoming with their time and money, their hand-me-downs, and their opinions—to know what to expect of their male offspring. After years of primary and secondary studies in one of the schools run by religious orders in the capital, these young men thought they no longer owed any dues to Quisqueyan society. A minority of them even made their way to the American school or the French lycée, though both were ostensibly reserved for the children of diplomats or foreign nationals. Then, a stint at a European university, either Swiss or French. Coursework completed or not, what difference did it make? Diplomas would serve at most to embellish their natural prerogatives as the sons of merchants or industrialists.

Their amorous declarations were halfway between melodrama and farce. They were never madly enough in love to flout the advice of the grandmother, custodian of the family traditions: "Never marry someone darker-skinned than your mother. Aim to father a generation whiter than your own." A notable exception was recognized where the dowry offered would compensate for the deficit in lighter-skinned babies! Even in those cases, however, it was necessary to weigh things carefully, to evaluate the pros and cons, so as not to place the family in an inferior position over the long run.

She understood these axioms so well that her smile glided

rapidly over the upper-class boys who craved impulsive flings or real romantic attachments, depending on their personalities, inhibitions, or culture. She ignored both types and kept a safe distance from them, too solicitous for her own future to let herself be taken in by the impromptu fabrications of reckless young men. Other suitors were pencil pushers, the plodding sons of the middle class condemned to toil away as bookkeepers in businesses owned by others or to shout themselves hoarse while standing in front of blackboards. Though bearing them no ill will, she trampled on their fawning gazes. She had no intention of enduring a dreary, hand-to-mouth existence, fixated on minimizing every expense, spending her nights tossing and turning with anxiety about the next day, bearing children condemned to replicate the same way of life in a perpetual downward spiral. When she was introduced to the young physician Fabien Doréval, she immediately recognized him as the person who would deliver her from all that. They shared the same imperatives, similar origins, and an all-consuming ambition.

« »

Since Wednesday, the nursing home has been under heightened security. An intruder, almost surely a Quisqueyan, skulked through the corridors, penetrating as far as the widow's room, and inserted his head through the half-open door. Blindly heeding the director's standing instructions, I hurried to close the door and chase away the intruder. But before he left, in a voice astonishingly spirited and forceful for someone who looked so droopy and timid, the man snarled at me, "So she, too, is going to die in her bed. Then there's no justice in this country!"

I can't forget his words; etched in my memory is the face of this man more ravaged by hurt and powerlessness than by anger. Do I have the right to ignore all those disfigured lives?

The temptation to act is growing stronger and stronger in my mind as I contemplate the old woman's dormant form. The idea has evolved as the weeks go by. I am seriously weighing its feasibility. What began as a cloudy speculation, born of my sorrow and frustrations, is becoming real. Martine, a Quisqueyan friend who has lived in France for more than twenty years, but who still believes strongly in the powers of the Vodou deities, often mentions a Quisqueyan *ougan* who resides in Paris and whose results she guarantees on the basis of her many experiences with him. It would be only fitting if the dictator's widow died at the hands of an *ougan*. The dictator who toyed so much with people's beliefs to entrench his rule! But I can't reconcile myself to such a solution. I can try to obtain toxic substances by other means. That would perhaps be harder, but it would still be doable. The prospect of my initiating any sort of punishment gives me a heady sensation, a novel one for me. I want to keep the idea simmering on the burner, not rush it. In any case, the old woman, bedridden, speechless, and impotent, has no escape.

« »

The memory of the betrayal still pained her as much as ever. A face with abhorrent features, pale eyes, and permanent-waved hair passed before her eyes. How could Fabien have become entranced by that woman, brought her into their household, spent hours with her under the pretext that she was serving as his private secretary? Every day, watching them sit side by side, like accomplices, touching each other, now whispering, now falling into silence. She was supposed to have accepted all that without reacting! The rival had thought she could consolidate her power by marrying her brother into the family as a replacement for Marie-Danielle's no-good husband. On the basis of soft caresses, wanton thighs, and overwrought embraces. But Odile could not let that woman walk all over her, and she would never abandon the family to her wiles. She and her eldest daughter had always understood each other. If she stood up for Marie-Danielle's husband (while not vouching at all for his character), if she supported that fast-talking con man, it was because she wanted to protect her daughter and the grandchildren and also deal a mortal blow to that woman. When, as a result of Odile's constant pressure on Fabien, the woman whom public rumor identified only by her married name—Madame Saint-Albain—finally left the country, it was one of the sweetest victories of her married life.

She would not have allowed Fabien to throw away all that

they'd been through together. Not that he had wanted to, but sometimes the cup reaches its limit and adding even a droplet causes it to overflow. A brief mention of the difficult years, of the period when rumors of impotence kept him in a semipermanent state of rage, was enough to remind him of his vulnerability. All men, regardless of their degree of intelligence, reveal themselves to be particularly susceptible to problems of that nature. As if on some level they defined themselves by that organ, by its functioning, its prowess or its inadequacy. She didn't complain, at least not overtly. With regard to her position as first lady, as she conceived of it, she played the game out of loyalty to her husband. Until the day he dared to raise his arm to strike her. Then and there, she forgot to modulate her voice, forgot to behave as a married woman, respectful and reserved . . . on that day only.

Some wives didn't share this sense of duty toward their husbands. On the contrary, they actively tried to destroy their partners. She saw an example of that in her own family, but years earlier she had abandoned all attempts to understand her son's marital situation. The relationship between a man and a woman must in any case remain uncharted territory. No one can intrude there without risk of being ridiculed, frustrated, or duped. In the end she swallowed her defeat but never hid her opinion of the Foreigner.

The wedding was one of the regime's greatest errors. She would remain convinced until the end—which was fast approaching—that this lavish display of eye-catching apparel and jewelry, this extravagant and provocative ceremony, had precipitated the regime's downfall. Right in the midst of a crisis, to scoff at the people and to impose on them the spectacle of this mulatto woman decked out in a white gown. A divorcée in white! What an outrage! For the bride to go so far as to order a fur coat and command the palace technicians to run the air-conditioning at full blast so that she could wear it. Then to prance around in front of the cabinet ministers, the army officers, the paramilitaries; to put on such a show in front of the soldiers who had left their wives in their sweltering quarters, with a sputtering fan as their only relief. Utter madness!

She had found it necessary to surround herself with loyalists; it was thanks to them that they were able to hold on for another fifteen years after Fabien's death. And yet once again popular opinion had predicted a reign of only a few months, asserting that the Heir couldn't hang on any longer than that.

Just as at the very beginning, when Fabien was ill. She recalled the chaos surrounding his heart attacks. The first one was a veritable nightmare! First of all, the shock, the consternation, the doctor's ineptitude. An incompetent who had made her spend hours in unforgettable anguish. How could she contemplate losing Fabien, after only two years in power, after just fifteen years of marriage, when her youngest, Jean-Paul, had just celebrated his seventh birthday? She was going to find herself widowed with children still in need of supervision and a father's presence. Had Fabien died, the debacle that followed his death would have brought down the regime and put in jeopardy the advances that were barely under way. Fortunately, he survived that first attack, no thanks to the doctors' expertise. Truly, those so-called specialists turned out to be worthless! She regarded Fabien's responses as very lenient: he merely dismissed the incompetents and shunted them aside. Had she been in his place, she might well have shown more severity. But at least that episode prepared her for the Deceased's other heart problems, his chest pains, mood swings, threats, and tirades.

《 》

Your mother knew so many stories of girls whose complexions were too dark, whose hair was too nappy, and who were denied admission on some pretext or other, that she refused to enroll you at the prestigious school on the Avenue Crown run by the Sisters of St. Joseph of Cluny—refused, she'd repeat to anyone who would listen, to subject you to that humiliation. You were accepted by the Sisters of Divine Wisdom, where you nonetheless associated with the daughters of the bourgeoisie—you always made a point of reminding me emphatically that in your day such a thing was still possible.

During my rare visits to Port-du-Roi, I observed the existence of diverse worlds that had almost nothing to do with each other, and on the few occasions they did, always in very specific contexts. Contacts were kept to a strict minimum. Even in the nightclubs where my cousins took me during our brief stays and where young people came to enjoy themselves. All privileged in one way or another in this wounded country, and yet they grouped themselves according to the color of their skin, their incomes, their proficiency in French. Everyone behaved as if this compartmentalization was normal. Boys and girls danced as if these obvious barriers represented something other than an insult to their country's history. Any mention of color prejudice was strictly taboo, for then a silence would descend, heavy with reproach. "We outgrew that kind of thing long ago!" And right away the slurs would rain down on anyone who risked challenging that assertion. And of course someone would bring up Doréval and the havoc he had wrought by raising "the question of color." Soon enough, there would be references to the little priest in the National Palace. No one had wanted to understand that both the dictator and the priest had only plunged the knife more deeply into a festering wound.

When I tried to broach those questions with you, you fell back on your personal experience as though it trumped everyone else's. And I had to listen once again to the story of your friendship with Laura, a former schoolmate, youngest daughter of a well-known mulatto mercantile family. You and Laura were best friends in the latter years of elementary school. "We used to share our most intimate secrets," you would murmur, as if forgetting that the opportunity for an adult friendship between the two of you turned out to be almost nonexistent. Your paths barely crossed again.

But I never dared contradict you. I masked every stirring of revolt, choked back every question that could have caused hurt, stifled the doubts that were poised on my lips.

I remember an incident in a store in Alexandreville during one of our brief visits to Quisqueya. You had dragged me there to buy the products of Quisqueyan artisans, justly renowned for their creativity and delicate craftsmanship. Around us were a fairly impressive number of other customers, considering the economy's fragility. Besides the locals, there were foreigners and expatriates like us, endowed with supercharged foreign currencies that made the proprietor's skirt twirl as she bustled to serve us. The ambience was polite, Frenchified, and rather standoffish. Luxury perfume floated in the air. The little bell on the door tinkled, and all eyes turned instinctively toward the new customer. A woman, simply dressed, her face slick with sweat, her expression sheepish in the face of so many glances. Each one astonished. Some indifferent, others unmistakably cold. The proprietor sized up the newcomer but gave no sign of welcome, returning her attention to customers who were worth her while. Nonetheless, animated by a sense of determination that was stronger than her apparent diffidence, the sweat-soaked woman advanced toward a sales clerk and murmured something to her. The clerk responded offhandedly and with a shrug that conveyed her disdain. I inwardly admired the courage of the intruder, who insistently repeated her question in a somewhat louder voice. She was speaking Creole, which turned heads a second time. It had to do with a gift she wanted for a cousin who was getting married in Boston and who had seen this item in the store. She tried to describe an iron sculpture of imposing appearance. Wanted to know if the store expected to obtain others in the same style. Wondered what it would cost. If it wasn't too expensive, she was eager to buy it for her cousin in Boston, because he was so kind. And her voice rose, her Creole blazed with her desire to show her gratitude to her cousin who had settled in America. Condescending smiles formed, eyebrows arched up. The proprietor then stepped forward. Her voice rang out like a slap. Patronizing, dismissive, brooking no appeal: "Madame, we told you we can't help you." The woman tried one last time to stammer out her story, but the proprietor's glare stopped the flow of words. The sweaty-faced woman finally went quiet. She backed away and exited.

I waited for one of the customers to react. I waited, Maman, for you to be the first to make the proprietor understand that she should have behaved civilly toward this woman, who only wanted to buy a gift for a relative, who had not offended the dignity of the nation by speaking Creole, and who was not responsible for the fact that she had no car and had perspired

under the broiling sun of Port-du-Roi. I would have been satisfied if you'd simply commented on the incident as we left the
store, if you'd linked it like so many others to the climate of
exclusion that relegated a large segment of the population to
circumscribed spaces, if you'd perhaps poured out your indignation with your customary verve—but the days went by with
no mention of the event. We left Quisqueya soon afterward.
Curiously, you never did speak of the woman dripping with
sweat.

<< >>

*On Sundays, when rumors of coups or conspiracies didn't
throw them into an anxious frenzy, the family sometimes went
to their property west of the capital. A place of simplicity, an in-
formal, less pretentious lifestyle. She felt good there. She would
let herself sink into one of the mahogany chairs, with classic
lines and a somewhat rigid back, but so similar to those of her
Tante Cléante that she always nestled into them with delight.
She struck up neighborly relations with the villagers, conducted
herself—oh! so effortlessly!—as a grand lady taking her leisure.*

*The bucolic environment brought back happy memories of
her family. The dinners on the last Sunday of the month at
Tante Cléante's, where her sisters and she would gather with
their relatives. In the early days of her marriage, she rarely
missed these get-togethers. She adored her sisters, even though
they didn't share her resentment toward their mother. The four
resembled each other to a degree that was striking for those
who knew of their diverse paternity, as if the paternal genes
had made no impact on the arrangement of their features. Or
perhaps their mother had chosen men who were all alike!*

*Peals of laughter and conversation, kitchen aromas, and
clinking glasses punctuated their gatherings in a convivial
atmosphere that was at once rustic and elegant. The reason,
no doubt, was that all the sisters took pleasure in sashaying
about in their exquisite apparel in this simple setting. And also
because the cousins, six girls and three boys, bickered good-
naturedly, combining ruggedly physical games with talkfests*

*and with fashion shows that the girls organized under the boys'
mocking eyes.*

*Fabien had always respected her sense of family and her
need to share her good fortune with her relatives. Her family
had benefited in every possible way from her position as first
lady. As soon as they'd finished secondary school, two of her
nieces went off to the same Swiss university as her daughters.
Her nephews all received cars as soon as they attained the legal
driving age—or even before. Indeed, Jean-Paul adored sports
cars and often gave them to his cousins. On many occasions,
she was forced to intercede with Fabien on behalf of cousins,
sons of cousins, and godsons implicated in prosaic dramas that
could have turned out badly.*

*Like the time one of her nephews, Philippe Moreau, had a
fling with his wife's younger sister. The two sisters, both pregnant
by the same man, lived for a time under the same roof. Philippe
had always been something of a daredevil, drawn to reckless
adventures and sticky situations. To assuage his father-in-law's
wrath, he presented the family with a 4 × 4 and two round-trip
plane tickets to the United States. The outraged father-in-law
threatened to kill him. How could she have remained indifferent to the justifiable panic of Angela, the youngest of her sisters,
who came to tell her the story? A squad of VSN thugs promptly
explained to the father-in-law that it would be best for him to
calm down and accept the reparations, and above all not to
make waves or spread the story around. If he did, he would
regret it. In the end, they all left the country: the two sisters,
the babies, and the in-laws. Philippe made no effort whatever to
retain them; it was obvious he didn't care about them. Several
months later, he admitted to his mother that the younger sister
was still a minor, but the outcome would have been the same in
any event. She could not decently have left him to the mercy of
the father's rage. You simply have to protect your own.*

*Likewise, she could not have tolerated her own sister pay-
ing the price for the impetuous actions of Léonard Daumier. It
was a pity that Clara didn't understand the motives behind the
regime's reaction. It pained Odile that her sister was still main-*

taining a cold and distant attitude after all this time. They'd been compelled to act quickly to make Clara divorce this man who was plotting against the government. Fabien had no choice but to come down hard on Daumier. She would never have believed that Clara's resentment would last so long. More than thirty years. Still, Clara had always been one to hold grudges. Even as an adolescent she would berate you for the most trivial remark a month after the fact. All the same, they used to get along well most of the time. Odile would have loved to see her sister again before it was too late. She felt time sliding between her thoughts as if it were playing hide-and-seek with her. Only she no longer had the strength to run after it, and above all she had no doubt which of the two would win the game.

She had always envisioned growing old with Fabien, like the elderly couples in her mother's native city, nodding off in rocking chairs on their sunlit stoops. Despite the first heart attack and her foretaste of separation, she fantasized for a long time about their twilight years of marital togetherness, a calm and fulfilling harvesttime. She used to dream of evenings with their grandchildren's laughter in the background, trips to Europe, shopping excursions to department stores. Of visits to countries they had never really found the time to explore. Her vision of retirement was the transfer of power to Marie-Danielle—or in a pinch to Jean-Paul once he'd matured sufficiently—from the hands of a Fabien who would be up in years but would govern until the transition was assured. A handover would be done in good and due form, not like what had actually happened, under conditions of anxiety and uncertainty.

Fabien hadn't made things any easier! Long refusing to envisage his inevitable death, he rejected all consideration of a successor. Proof that even the greatest sometimes have their blind spots! He saw himself as president forever, even though the doctors had written him off. The 1964 constitution made no provision for succession. She finally managed to convince him that it was preferable to create a plan, rather than put in jeopardy the revolution for which he'd sacrificed so much. But he remained dead set on the choice of Jean-Paul, whereas the most logical solution was to designate Marie-Danielle to

*take over. After all, their eldest daughter was already governing
while her father's latest illness kept him bedridden. The circumstances allowed Marie-Danielle to impose her domineering
personality and exercise her managerial skills. And yet Fabien
would hear none of it. Odile had exhausted herself in trying
to persuade him to pass the torch before it was too late. She
reluctantly decided she'd be going too far if she also made him
accept Marie-Danielle. Besides, she had to wonder whether the
Quisqueyan public was ready for such a choice.*

*In the end, Fabien didn't have much trouble winning ac-
ceptance for his son. "Young people of my country," he said,
"here is the young leader I promised you." He had set his right
hand on Jean-Paul's shoulder, and that photo was circulated all
around the country and soon all around the world. Once again,
constitutional amendments were quickly enacted to change the
age of eligibility for the presidency from thirty-five to nineteen.
Then, the referendum of January 30 recorded 2,390,816 votes
in favor of Fabien's choice and none opposed. In less than two
months Fabien had organized everything necessary for the transition to pass off without a hitch.*

*It took her much longer than that to get used to his absence,
to the void created by all that she missed: the measured cadences
of his voice, the muffled tread of his steps. The children, particularly the younger ones, were inconsolable, weeping without
shame, but for her it was as if she had been condemned to live
with a part of herself brutally torn away. From time to time she
groped toward the missing part, but she was never able to catch
hold of the shreds. All those years lived with another, only to
find herself suddenly alone. At the end of her life, her loneliness
seemed even more unbearable to her.*

« »

You sometimes spent hours on end describing the wedding
of Jean-Paul and Isabelle and the reactions evoked by the an-
nouncement. They varied from the most fatalistic indifference
to the most vehement indignation. At a time when the country
was floundering in poverty, people were starving to death, the
value of the coffee crop was falling by the day, and the country's

economy was becoming ever more dependent on foreign aid, this idiot was marrying a scion of the bourgeoisie. He had just slaughtered the country's pigs to prevent a supposedly imminent epidemic. The Americans had demanded it, and of course Baby Fab knuckled under. He didn't protect the country. Outsiders accused us of spreading AIDS and all sorts of other diseases, and he didn't object. Though the brightly colored posters of the Office of Tourism still blithely proclaimed, *"Vive la Différence!,"* tourists no longer set foot here.

Heated discussions flared up between the old-timers who missed Fabien and the apologists for his son. "Jean-Paul didn't even choose someone with money. Instead, he's going for a gold-digger, a divorcée who's only marrying him to grab a pile of his cash. A Sunday, no less; the Lord's Day. One more sacrilege. Ah! He's not like his father. Fabien would never have accepted this marriage."

"What are you talking about, you moron? Wasn't it your Papa Fab who sided with the Americans against Castro and who gave huge privileges to bourgeois fat cats for cooperating with him? You seem to forget he gave that German industrialist Kurt Holsen exclusive rights to import fabric and finished goods. Who did his youngest daughter marry? And who was his chosen mistress? So why should only the son bear the burden of their hypocrisy?"

The crowd had gathered very early in front of the cathedral. This time it wasn't necessary to send trucks into the countryside to round up droves of peasants. The petit bourgeoisie, no less than the middle class and the elite, wanted to watch the festivities. The laborers, the small-time vendors, the whole lower-class world of Port-du-Roi scurried there to take in the wedding of the century. The bride's hair drawn back to prop up her gigantic headdress and flatter her skillfully made-up eyes, the groom's gold chain and rings, his solemn countenance, which was more contrived than authentic: these and other details of the wedding, large and small, were dissected and analyzed. The government released an official photo that was published throughout the world. It wasn't every day that a country with such a paltry per-capita income spent five million dollars to show off a new presidential couple. That's without regard to the prenuptial frivolities and those that would come later. Jean-Paul's million-dollar yacht, for one. The young Madame Isabelle Baudet Doréval adored splurging on jewelry, designer apparel, and gaudy shoes. She was given to parading around in front of people, both men and women.

Sometimes I tried in vain to dam the torrent of your words. To discredit your chronology and force you to confront the fateful year and the enforced silence that surrounded it. The year of my father's death, the year of our departure for Martinique, before your dark vision permanently colored my own view of the world.

I methodically reviewed my notes on the Doréval regime. My contact with the widow plunged me willy-nilly into that period. It seemed a worthy occasion to reread the notebooks covered with your crabbed handwriting and to revise my own scribblings. On my computer, I opened new folders in the big Doréval file and keyed in your notes and mine. In the evenings, I went to bed exhausted and slept fitfully. Often I woke up sweating in the middle of the night. Sometimes the name that was so well known came unwilled to my lips: Odile Savien Doréval. I savored the richness of the syllables within my mouth. With a mixture of fascination and resentment. Also of self-loathing, for after my assigned work is done, I have difficulty curbing the impulses that propel me toward the widow's bed in that boxy room whose pastel-colored walls can't conceal the moribund atmosphere.

My mind reels, torn between recollection and reality, besieged by your nightmares and my own aspirations.

« »

From their very first meeting, she realized that she would marry Fabien. She had been without any romantic involvement for two years, having moved quickly to break up with that engineer from Nippes. The openly scornful looks of his mother and sisters told her clearly that, as a modest young nurse, she did not measure up to the expectations of this petit bourgeois family aspiring to improve its social status. She would have simply laughed this off if the engineer's character had not seemed so contemptible to her. Lacking both strength and determination. Deficient in both courage and dignity. She could never have spent her life with such a mediocre individual. She broke up with him three months after their first date. Thereafter, she waited, hoping to find a man capable of meeting her requirements, strong enough not to be frightened by her ambitions. When she saw Fabien and met his gaze, it was the beginning of their shared drama. A story of love and power, respect and tenderness. A journey that was sometimes difficult but always passionate.

"Odile, my faithful and tireless companion." He often mentioned her in his speeches and writings. Talked with her about decisions he had to make. Listened to her even when their opinions differed. Shared with her the ecstasy of power. She couldn't fail to lend a hand when troubles mounted up. She had come into their marriage with settled ideas about the masculine gender, strongly influenced by the misdeeds of her father, who had served as a symbol of callous male behavior. Beyond that, the experiences of several of her women friends had revealed on various occasions how vile and debased men can be. At best, she only half-trusted them, always primed to resist their treachery. With Fabien, she had gradually lowered her guard, for they shared so many experiences. But her watchful and secretive side had reemerged when she realized he was interested in someone else and even ready to ally with the woman and her family against his own children. Oh, but he was! For all her respect for him, she would not let herself be taken for a fool.

In this, she was unlike the chatty confidante of her youthful days, Thérèse Bouchette, a nurse of baffling serenity. Thérèse admitted to her colleagues that she climbed into bed each night beside her husband, a maniac who kept a knife stashed under his pillow and threatened to skewer her liver with it. And that she was able to fall asleep without difficulty. "What do you expect me to do?" Thérèse would ask in her placid voice. "If he really wants to kill me, do you think I'll be able to stop him?"

Once in power, Odile almost regretted that she had never dealt with her friend's husband. Meanwhile, in fact, Thérèse's parents had gotten rid of him, literally buying her a divorce. Odile would gladly have settled the man's fate.

She had heard plenty of stories about cheating and violent husbands of all ages. Always fibbing to their wives, taking their pleasure elsewhere, fathering children outside the marriage with no thought of the consequences. On that score, she had no cause to reproach Fabien. In any case, just like her, he had too much regard for his reputation and his progeny to propagate them hither and yon.

« »

There it is, then. I feel liberated from my indecision. For the last two days I've been conducting serious research. I'm sleeping better. Will the prospect of action alleviate my nightmares? I'm so immersed in information about poisons—their effects, the time of action, the dosage for each substance—that I barely have time to think of anything else. When I look at the old woman, planning and theorizing replace anger and hatred. I feel more upbeat, less jittery. I approach the days with less dejection, the nights with more tranquility. Even my mental forays into the past have become less destructive.

« »

With a painful effort, the old woman managed to hold back the sigh that seemed intent on escaping from an unexpected place in her chest. The young woman was spying on her more and more. Even with her eyes closed, Odile could sense the hatred radiating from her. She would have to redouble her prudence and maintain her enervated appearance. She caught her sigh in the back of her throat and forced it down with a renewed twinge of the pain that never fully left her. She had never learned how to prepare herself for death. Refused to think about it. Preferred to cope with the realities of life without looking ahead to the moment when her body would abandon her. How hard it is, though, to look at yourself honestly!

« »

Shortly before your death—had you felt it coming?—you renewed your formerly close ties with some cousins who still lived in Quisqueya. From your bungalow in the Lamentin district or from the department store in the city center where, until your illness struck, you carried out the duties of a floor manager, you used to stay informed about "current affairs." You followed the changes that were occurring at a breakneck pace in Quisqueyan society. Curiously, you disregarded certain aspects, as if it hurt you too much to focus on them, and yet you lingered over others that seemed painful in their own right. For example, you refused to comment on the fact that a fairly large number of women were bleaching their skin, whereas you lamented the destruction of neighborhoods you had known. "So many ravages at every level," you told me with tears in your eyes, "and I can attest that they are solely responsible." I didn't need to ask who "they" were.

Any little thing could provoke a volley of ire and outrage. Your routine contacts with a compatriot at her new stall in the Fort-de-France marketplace never failed to bring you distressing news. "The state of the high schools has gotten even worse since the Doréval regime, can you believe it? That woman's nephew is in a tenth-grade classroom that has more than a hundred students piled on top of one another. I can't even imagine it." A telephone call from Port-du-Roi would throw you into an alarming frenzy. "Corruption is more rampant than ever. People have to pay bribes for the smallest service. And to think that they expected things to be better with the little priest! How ironic! People are still looking for a savior. They got a wolf in sheep's clothing." Or you'd burst into my bedroom after the evening news, full of indignation over the frosty reception given to your countrymen in the French Antilles. You lashed out against the unequal relationship between the developing countries and the rich ones. You worked yourself into a state over signs of intrusion in Quisqueyan affairs by certain powerful countries. I knew that no response would be adequate. I simply had to let the flood of words run its course, while putting on a look of dismay—meanwhile curbing my frustration and my urge to scream at you to knock it off.

I regret my cowardly inability to talk back to you. I settled for a spongelike passivity, my only use being to absorb a sea of regrets and gory stories. Instead, I should have helped you move beyond your history.

According to Latifa, with all the wisdom of her graduate studies in social psychology, you latched onto me so as not to topple over into insanity. "You were only a child," she reminded me. "How can a kid of six, ten, or even fifteen help an adult cope with her past and live her life differently? I know you adored your mother, Marie-Ange, but you have to recognize that she used you to keep from going crazy. I don't know whether she succeeded, but she certainly didn't spare you."

Latifa's words seemed to me somewhat unjust and oversimplified. No doubt she was partially correct, but how can anyone remake history? How can I be angry with you when I know what you lived through? How can I not share your past and your desperation?

« »

Fabien's dalliance nearly destroyed the family. She found herself torn between her children and their father. Protective mother, rebellious wife. A period of insomnia, chronic indigestion, nonexistent sexual appetite, and unrelenting rage. Her resentment toward Fabien assumed ever greater proportions, verging on the incurable, and her anger vied with her fear of losing the attributes that made them a strong couple and the envy of their opponents. The discussions between them multiplied, grew heated. For the first time Fabien made a hostile movement, the memory of which still caused a tingling sensation behind her eyelids.

She hadn't let herself be pushed around, however. She had fought, threatened, wielded all available weapons. Among them, words that struck at the most vulnerable part of his being, where men want to feel secure, surrounded by tenderness and clarity. She attacked his male pride, was upset with herself for doing so, but to protect her children she would have done it as often as necessary. She read the rancor in his eyes, saw his fists clench with rage. She felt it in her core, but she held firm.

She fought with the strength of a woman who knew her man intimately, knew his faults and his flash points, what tempted and what elated him. She folded those things, twisted them and hung them around his neck. It was too bad if in the course of the exercise she, too, had been badly bruised, leaving their marital rift marked indelibly on her heart.

She never stopped loving him, never regretted marrying him, but in rare moments, she hated him intensely.

« »

That boneheaded director just complimented me for overcoming my initial "animosity" and "acting like a professional worthy of this establishment." What drivel! I looked at him and nodded without further comment. He can take that any way he wants.

« »

She dressed in black for the funeral. The crepe veil around her head gave her profile the dignity of a grief-stricken but noble widow. Later, when she studied the photos, she felt such pride that she experienced the usual reflexive desire to share her satisfaction with Fabien. Then the stinging realization of his absence struck her, as it did numerous times over the course of the year following his demise. While on the one hand she was fighting against enemies within her circle—the self-styled comrades, the self-proclaimed friends of the revolution—on the other she was battling the perennial detractors, who were already rejoicing at the prospect of an unavoidable debacle. Every corner of the country was in ferment. Overseas, the eternal exiles, the habitual troublemakers, pooled their resources in dingy basement apartments in Brooklyn and Queens to support ridiculously small factions and sow disorder in the country once again.

Every kind of conjecture and supposition erupted regarding who would lead, who would emerge with a tight grip on power. As if she were only an incorporeal shadow, an outline without content. She would never let anyone outside the family benefit from Fabien's work. To the end, she carried out her duty as wife and mother. Propped up Jean-Paul, who needed it, though all the same, he was not the buffoon that the public imagined. Far from it! A son of theirs could not have lacked intelligence! But predators and vultures surrounded them. The Deceased would have been gratified to see the clear-sightedness and cunning she displayed in foiling intrigues and double-dealing, ignoring rumors and ploys, yielding neither to pressures nor to panic, standing up to the long-frustrated plotters who had dreamt even under Fabien of one day seizing the reins and believed she could be easily manipulated.

During all that time, she also had to cope with her grief. "I share your pain, Madame President," they would say to her stiffly. With handshakes, kisses, hugs. "Our sympathies in these painful circumstances." Pain, grief, sympathy. Formulaic phrases inadequate to characterize the desolation that was shattering her limbs.

Evenings. When the children, the relatives, the true friends returned to their homes, when all the vultures fluttered away, alone in her bed, she nursed her wounds. Let her tears flow everywhere. Her entire body would sob, not just her eyes, but also her arms that twitched like damaged limbs in search of restraints, her legs that the Deceased had often brushed lightly while pretending not to touch them at all, and most of all her hands, blind and bereft, which would reach in vain for the other body.

She was careful to make the funeral reflect the great man's importance. First of all, she had a gold cross placed on the pillow, near his left ear. His exemplary Autobiography of a Third World Leader, *which he would often leaf through to extract quotations, was likewise in plain view on the left side. She did not remove his glasses. They were an integral part of his personality, his image. To the end, she remained loyal, faithful, carrying herself erect and strong. A one-hundred-and-one-gun salute and the bells of all the churches in the country for the man who had dedicated his life to it. Her eyes grew misty during the service. In spite of herself, she stumbled and almost fell, but managed to regain her balance. To the end, standing proud and tall. Twenty-two officers and twenty-two enlisted men saluted her husband's passing. The end of fourteen years in power and twenty-two years of married life. Together, they brought four*

children into the world. It's too bad if Marie-Danielle wore an
indifferent expression and if Jean-Paul seemed to sink into his
chair. Nadine and Ti Odile mourned their father.

Then, suddenly, nature itself decided to remind the country
and the world that an illustrious figure was taking his leave.
A mysterious gust passed across the site, impetuous and un-
expected, ruffling the women's hair, lifting skirts and dresses,
making the bravest men shiver. Apparently, a number of
mourners darted into the covered spaces for protection. Then,
just as suddenly, the wind abated. She didn't really witness the
incident, for at that moment the tears were blinding her behind
her veil. Her sisters reported it to her, her friends told her about
it, and she read about it in foreign newspapers. The Deceased
had manifested himself forcefully even after his death.

« »

On the day of Fabien Doréval's funeral, you would have
thought that even the dictatorship would take a rest, that the
VSN would stop their blindly repressive practices, too shaken
by their leader's death to think about drawing their guns. And
yet, on the very day of the funeral, it was Marcel Bouvier's turn
to disappear, dragged away by the Tonton Macoutes. In the
days following the funeral, innumerable family conversations
were fueled by the tale of the wind that had come from the
great beyond to spread panic all through the funeral cortege.
Recounted in a thousand versions, it made incredulous listeners
laugh and more gullible ones tremble or cringe.

But not many Quisqueyans spoke of the very last murder attributable to Fabien Doréval, en route to his final resting place.
For me, however, the story symbolizes more than any other
the cruelty unleashed by a regime for which human life had no
importance.

On the way to the Port-du-Roi cemetery, the funeral cortege
passed in front of Marcel Bouvier's house. As soon as the con-
voy had passed, Marcel's mother, Madame Bouvier, eighty-six
years old, threw some water from her stoop. It was the time-
honored Quisqueyan method for warding off evil spirits and
cleansing the air of maledictions and sorcery. Spies reported

her action to the militia. A few hours later, the VSN showed up at the Bouviers' house. Marcel was playing cards with friends in the rear courtyard. He was arrested and then went missing. Never to be seen again. Like so many others.

The Quisqueyans who had settled in Martinique well before Jean-Paul Doréval's rise to power told of how they had rejoiced upon hearing of the older dictator's demise. They had spilled out into the streets singing and dancing. Broke out the bottle of five-star rum received as a Christmas gift. All their hopes of returning home—long hidden in a suitcase under the bed, in the back of a closet, or on a cupboard shelf—burst forth, riotous and impatient to be aired. Their hopes of escaping their present-day humiliations in a foreign land, of forgetting the wounds of a terror-filled past. Some immediately bought one-way tickets, while others more prudently tried to contact relatives still in Quisqueya to verify the news. To take the pulse of the mother country. They had fled from your island's four corners, its nine departments, all scarred by the dictatorship in their lives and memories. Some elderly people originally from Cap-Créole, alluding to the Bouvier case, recalled the practice, so common in their locale, of pouring out water after the passage of a funeral cortege. Especially if the altar boy, worried about getting too far ahead of the hearse, stopped and set down the base of the cross to rest his arms. Even if only for a moment! If by some mischance the cross had touched the ground in front of your house, it was imperative, in order to avert otherwise certain doom, to throw out some water as soon as the procession had passed. This prevented a death in the family, since the cross on the ground was the deceased's way of designating someone to follow him. Hadn't Madame Bouvier simply wanted to protect her household, her family?

So many men and women had been lost just as pointlessly, in equally banal ways. The city of Cap-Créole had borne its share of losses. And could we say anything different about Belle-Anse? Don't forget the South, where every stream carries drops of blood to the sea. The ridges of Grande-Plaine still echo with stories of corpses dragged from the hills to the highway and left there to show the punishment that awaited troublemakers. All the émigrés clustered around radios, televisions, and telephones to spread and share the news and replenish their longings with hope. While still nurturing their resentment.

One Sunday morning at Cap-Créole, the local militia commander ordered a school principal to open the doors of his establishment. Their informants had reported that an armed rebel was hidden there. The militiamen pulled the principal out of church, where he was attending Mass, and escorted him to his house to obtain the keys to the school. They found no one in the school, however. Apparently, the rebel had taken refuge in his attic. He emerged from his hiding place and surrendered just as the uniformed men were about to drag away his pregnant wife in reprisal.

At l'Anse-aux-Rocs, an illiterate promoted by Fabien Doréval to the post of regional commandant, in recognition of his loyalty and his expertise in torturing resisters, required all the inhabitants to stand at their windows or on their balconies to salute him when he entered the town. Whether it was three in the afternoon, Saturday at dinnertime, or Friday in the middle of the night, he had to be met with the citizens' cheers and applause. Woe to any resident who didn't light a candle quickly enough or turn on a lamp—if by some stroke of luck there was electricity. Savage retribution awaited them. As accompaniments to all these dismal stories, sighs mingled with nodding heads and the clearing of throats.

« »

She poured herself into the completion of the mausoleum. Met the architect personally, chose the white marble, the simple yet elegant designs, the layout. It seemed to her that she was prolonging her contact with Fabien by lingering over the details, the plans and drawings that the architect submitted to her. She supervised the construction of the edifice and ordered the flowers for its inauguration. She told herself that she would go there to join him in thirty years or more, because in her family the women rarely died before eighty! Later, in Paris, she was stunned and devastated to learn that a raging mob had destroyed the mausoleum and ransacked the tomb in search of

Fabien Doréval's body. As if she would have left her husband's remains to their mercy! In 1964, the family of Claude Joris had "put away" his body to prevent his enemies from using it—Fabien had become aware of that when his henchmen had brought him the casket on the day of Joris's funeral. She, too, had subsequently considered the possibility that someone would want to snatch her husband's brain. No, she couldn't say she had imagined the horror that transpired, this avalanche of violence and savagery, the desecration of the tombs and the mausoleum, this barbaric outburst she had watched on the French TV networks. Still, she had taken the necessary measures to protect him against all attempts at zombification,* against any possible intention to defile his remains. She had summoned Zacharie, the grand ougan. *With more than usual attentiveness, she followed all his orders, took care to satisfy his every request. This wasn't Zacharie's first visit to the palace, nor his last. He didn't stint on his services—or his time or expertise, either. The necessary arrangements were made not only to put Fabien Doréval's body in a secure place, but also to prevent anyone from using his brain.*

She had confidence in Zacharie, since he had never disappointed her all through the years when she and Fabien so often consulted him before making decisions. With faith in Zacharie's know-how, but also to foster the public perception that they enjoyed a privileged rapport with the ougans *and an advanced acquaintance with Vodou, its power and lore. A perception carefully nurtured by Fabien. At the outset, she winced when he ordered that ceremonies be conducted within the palace compound by Zacharie or sometimes by Marianne, a celebrated* mambo* *of southern origin. Then she herself was initiated into the ritual and gradually became involved in the preparations from the* jetedlo* *until the final sacrifice. She knew where to place the various objects, including the smoked glass bottles and the calabashes full of snake vertebrae. Mentally noted the significance of different-colored candles. Was particularly fond of the purple one for its help in times of danger for her family or friends. Over the years she had lit several purple candles to free herself from malevolent forces in such situations. In a* *general way, she was intoxicated by the mysterious atmosphere of the rituals. By the scent of burning wax, the imposing majesty of the* poteau mitan,* *and the stunning intricacy of the* vévés.* *Just as she was moved at Catholic services, despite the large number of interminable liturgies she had attended as first lady. She couldn't resist the subdued but profound pleasure of repeating the words of the liturgy, pronounced the celebrant's words along with him: "Peace be with you," and murmured the responsive phrase with complete naturalness: "And with your spirit. Amen."*

« »

I'm envisioning alternatives to poison. This morning, as I made the widow's bed, my hand grazed the pillow. I plumped and smoothed it. Of course, smother her! Undoubtedly the easiest solution, requiring the least preparation. Simply wait for the opportune moment and seize it. Don't hesitate, concentrate on the regime's victims while doing the deed. Besides, it would be soon be over, a simple pressure of the hands. Given the old woman's condition, who would be surprised?

« »

They were married, she and Fabien, on a December day in the cathedral of Port-du-Roi. The flourishing poinsettias gave the city a festive air. She had always relished the mildness of December. In contrast to Fabien, who preferred the month of April, between the reborn verdure of March and May's abundant blooms. She lulled herself in the coolness of the year's final month, the month of good luck baths *and red Christmas decorations, a month that dazzles with its passion and fervor. The closer one gets to its end, the more luminous the air becomes. Like a long, resplendent scarf whose end tickles like a farewell.*

« »

Why did you always save for last the stories of resistance and of revenge against the VSN, after all the accounts of repression and torture? Perhaps to remind me that life can outfox even the high and mighty? On one occasion they came to arrest a middle school teacher in a small northwestern city, and the principal stalled them in his office while his wife took women's clothing to the male teacher, who blended in with the kitchen staff. The militiamen failed to discover the ruse and left in a rage. To show their displeasure, they fired shots in the air, terrifying the students.

Under Fabien Doréval, no one could leave the country without authorization from the regime. The names of dissidents were recorded on a list, and members of a special team of inspectors automatically blocked them at the airport. Sometimes an unlucky person was turned back simply because his first and last names matched those of an enemy of the regime appearing on the famous list. In the time it took to verify his identity, he missed his flight and experienced hours or days of uncertainty. Nevertheless, for a whole year a clandestine network of dissidents and veterans had access to the seals authorizing departure from the country. They established contacts among the airport staff and even managed to alter the list that the dictator's spy services had arbitrarily compiled. As a result, many individuals escaped who would otherwise have had to live underground and at constant risk.

In the Martaban quarter, the capital's southern suburb, a group of young men fired on an especially bloodthirsty militiaman who was spreading terror among local families. The shots missed him, but for days the VSN militiamen, panic-stricken, would go out only when they were heavily reinforced. In addition, popular songs rang out everywhere, full of defiant humor. Secretly mocking the torturers. Jokes and anecdotes targeting the most notorious Doréval loyalists circulated from house to house, enlivening meetings of friends, who repeated them in whispers. One such anecdote concerned the slap that Fabien gave Lambert Chambral in the midst of a cabinet meeting and the degrading reaction of Lambert, who murmured, "Forgive me, Excellency!" How shameful!

It was in the retelling of such stories that many émigrés as homesick as you passed their years of exile. Except when they were trying to renew their residency cards, apply for menial jobs, or pursue other dead ends, because they had to start all over again as if they hadn't already paid their dues in life. Always in the backs of their minds were their memories of an oppressive past, from which they could hope to break free only with great turmoil and agitation.

« »

She no longer remembered the previous Christmas with her children. How your memory plays tricks on you when it teams up with old age! The hymns learned at the orphanage and the accompanying taste of hot chocolate invaded her senses. A chocolate that was not especially smooth, with an excess of sugar and cinnamon to cover the paucity of milk and cocoa: that was what her memory offered to her. How empty all that seemed!

« »

Since Monday, the nursing home's social coordinator has had Christmas music playing softly in the corridors. This struck me as a pathetic gesture. I don't know whether it's meant to remind the patients of the departed pleasures of yesteryear or to inspire them to take advantage of the holiday season, which is undoubtedly their last. Judging from the absence of visitors, there is every likelihood that the old lady will spend the holidays alone in the depressing sterility of her room.

I miss you more than ever, Maman. Is it from seeing this solitary woman at the end of her life and knowing how much I would have loved to have you with me? How will I spend New Year's Day, my first one without you? Without the cake you used to bake every year? Or that famous consommé you made from your grandmother's recipe? You began simmering the bouillon on New Year's Eve, with all the manner of a light-hearted little girl. At sunrise the next morning, the mouth-watering aroma would search me out in my bedroom. Never failing to offer visitors a bowl, you explained to them that this was a Quisqueyan tradition. In the late afternoon, when we were starting to forget the numerous lunch courses and our appetites were slowly returning, we would sit down to a slice of upside-down cake, accompanied by a cup of coffee. The coffee of our island, the best. I used to repeat with you: the best. How can I spend the first day of the year without you?

And yet I feel you close to me, your expression slightly ironic and also a wee bit impatient, but always full of tenderness and affection. I have reconnected with our part of the island, and I find you there alive and very active. I regularly receive news from the relatives and friends living in Quisqueya with whom you had stayed in contact. For me, that began as a simple act of courtesy. With my reply to an e-mail, and then gradually my attitude passed from mild annoyance, adroitly concealed—you know how skilled I am at hiding my feelings!—to a growing interest. In spite of myself, I compared the Quisqueyans' lives to those of the young people in Martinique. Just as you used to do when I was growing up, surrounded by madras clothing and the local Creole music, attracted by the shopping centers and the new little Renault I just had to have, no matter what it cost, and the latest high-tech gadget you forced me to explain while you pretended not to understand. Still, I refused at first to let myself be dragged into those never-ending dramas of visas to be obtained for the Quisqueyans who counted on you, of medical bills and school tuition to be paid. Taking on all those problems left you broke and mentally exhausted. I tried to resist the abyss of knotty problems, the morass of difficulties with their thorny tangles.

But what drew me inexorably were the silences, the ellipses and dead spaces, the voids infiltrated by a mute perplexity. The moments of drift in which despair overpowers all of life and stifles all expression. Sometimes in boys and girls younger than I. It was their youth that swayed me toward them. Without even being aware of it, I opened myself to their lives. I now send and receive e-mails, call them on the phone. I can't remain indifferent to the urge to be alive that wells up in them, some-times unexpectedly. A powerful gust of hope and courage that defies all obstacles and seems ready to engulf me, too. These contacts throw me into a world where reality nudges me along and shakes up my memory. As if I were emerging slowly from a long, hazy tunnel.

The notes of "Vive le vent d'hiver," a seasonal song set to a jazzy arrangement, float through the building. The frenetic atmosphere outside, the images of light-strung streets, bedecked storefronts, and gift-wrapped packages lend a surreal character to this drab room where silence broods in every corner. More than ever, the motionless form on the bed seems to interrogate me. I move closer to it in spite of myself, watching closely for some slim sign of cognition in the weary features. I wordlessly summon her to face up to me and answer my questions, to state her name before a tribunal, her hand raised in an oath of truthfulness, and to confront justice and her memory. I lower my gaze toward the bed, and a lucid glance meets mine. As if to forestall my instinctive movement of rejection, a hand grasps my arm. Swiftly, as if retreating from an observed danger, I free myself and back away. But before reaching the door, I think I hear a raspy croak coming from the bed, a hesitant, quavering appeal: "Marie-Ange."

Odile sees marie-Ange and says
she's unisqnean

FOUR

THE WOMAN AND THE SURVIVOR

*She no longer remembered her age. She had hidden it so well
all her life. Ever since adolescence, first as a coy flirtation, and
then, over the years, out of habit. And now she is losing her way
in the thousand detours of a tired brain. All her energy was con-
centrated on peering into the corners of her mind, on not letting
go. She couldn't recall whether she was born in 1913 or 1914.
The Deceased had been ten years older than she, or was that
an invention he went along with and repeated to anyone who
cared to listen? What did it matter, apart from the need to put
your finger on details suddenly deemed important out of a sheer
desire for control? Whether she was eighty-four or eighty-two
changed nothing of the reality that her life was ebbing away.
Like a faucet that's wearing out, it's useless to turn it off more
tightly, there's no stopping the slow drip that's so annoying to
hear. In this establishment where death so often dislodged life,
no one else was attending to the sounds of her life leaving.*

*Except perhaps that young woman with the sad, heavy-
lidded eyes. In fact, Odile was beginning to get used to the aide's
piercing stare that contrasted so strangely with her calm and assured behavior. The days she didn't come seemed much longer
to Odile, too much like death and the eternal silence—despite
her decision to still her own voice. What was making her listen
for Marie-Ange's footsteps? Was it perhaps her ultimate need
of being, if not loved, then at least understood? Why had she
given in to that overpowering impulse to murmur the girl's first
name? For some time she had felt less threatened, or perhaps it
was that, not being able to confront the young woman directly,
she had adapted to her latent hostility. Instinctively, Odile knew
that Marie-Ange came from Quisqueya, not from the French
Antilles. And yet she did not have a Quisqueyan accent. In her*

brief conversations with other caregivers, she used the expres-
sions of the young students of the Parisian region. She would
check her cell phone, continually fiddle with a little gadget she
carried in her pocket, mention her credit card, and like so many
others of her generation, she seemed to suffer from anorexia or
some other eating disorder. Nevertheless, Odile had immedi-
ately detected a Quisqueyan background behind her outward
appearance as a young woman from mainland France. Prob-
ably in her gait! Those buttocks that cause a swishing sound as
they rub against the fabric of her skirt or slacks, those gently
swaying hips that invite attention, and that movement of the
shoulders at once languid and deliberate. In her expression,
also—proud, unyielding. Or was Odile trying to visualize her-
self as youthful and sporty again, like this young woman who
undoubtedly hated her without even knowing her?

« »

I detest death. It's been around us all my life, invading our
slightest movements. Unknown dead people dominated my
childhood and adolescence. All those anonymous fatalities I
mourned. Family members with frozen expressions in yellowed
family photos. I abhor the atmosphere in which you raised
me—oozing with fear and regret, anger and powerlessness,
with unfinished farewells forever dangling. An atmosphere de-
vouring every intention I had of living happily. Swallowing up
all my possibilities of pleasure and joy.

I detest this dour gravity I inherited from you. This glum-
ness that, according to you, settled permanently in the family
with Jean-Édouard's passing. A young man barely nineteen.
Feisty and fearless, ready for action. After the public execution of the two dissidents against the wall of the Port-du-Roi
cemetery, your brother changed. His once-contagious liveliness
dimmed. He became secretive and taciturn, slow and deliberate in his movements. Oddly reassured, your mother believed
he had settled down. He was coming home earlier than usual,
no longer staying out to wander around with his neighborhood
pals, skirting dangerously close to the curfew hour. Avoiding
the enforcement sweeps that could result in a trip to the near-

est police station and a brutal beating, if not much worse. His parents thought that on his rare evenings out he was dutifully reviewing his notes with fellow students in preparation for the coming academic term, his first year of law school. It was only when the Dorévalist police raided the local branch of the PPPL and arrested its leaders that your parents learned of their son's recent enlistment in the party ranks. Every week he attended consciousness-raising sessions there, led by an eminent history professor known for his revolutionary ideas. Jean-Joseph Desravines Aubert and his wife Laurette were taken into custody on the day of the raid. Lengthening the list of murder victims. Jean-Édouard returned to your house, frantic with excitement. Explained to your terrified parents that he had to go underground, that the police were investigating and pursuing everyone connected with the party.

That was the very last time you saw your big brother. He would never again pull your braids the way he so often did to tease you. His slightly panicked yet resolute expression glided over your father, your mother, and lingered a moment on you, the little sister. Like a tender, emotional snap of his fingers. He left the house and never came back alive. Two days later your parents retrieved his body at Fort Décembre. Officially, the guards had been forced to shoot the prisoner as he tried to escape.

« »

When she received her first paycheck as a nurse, she ordered two new dresses for herself. She insisted that the dressmaker follow the patterns perfectly, with an impeccable cut, precise and classic lines. She despised cheap clothing, preferring to invest in high-quality fabric rather than settle for skirts that frayed after two launderings. Buying clothes consumed all of her savings, sometimes amassed by literally depriving herself of all nonessentials and by walking even during heat waves to save the cost of public transport or taxis. Her clear and detailed requests on matters of fashion were a topic of conversation for the local seamstresses and dressmakers. Some were reluctant to accept her orders, since the fittings dragged on for so long and

*always led to alterations. But she invariably came away satis-
fied. Never would she accept an inferior piece of work. Years
later, the staff at the National Palace would grumble that she
was overly meticulous and had luxurious tastes. Believing, no
doubt, that her position as first lady had gone to her head.*

*A perfect appearance. That was always her motto. She wasn't
going to fall short of it under the pretext of economizing for the
government, while all around them supporters of the revolution
were stuffing their pockets and their bank accounts and corrupt
hacks were building stately mansions with public resources.*

*Of course, Fabien sometimes chose not to intervene. Not
because he longed to be appreciated, but to assure the loyalty
of his most competent subordinates. No investment was more
solid than a carefully measured sharing of resources with true
and devoted underlings. On the one hand, the most severe punishment for traitors, and on the other, protection and generosity
toward the most loyal. As a result, Fabien was invariably fore-
warned of attempted conspiracies, the slightest hint of restive-
ness within the army or among the cabinet ministers. Naturally,
he often had to differentiate unfounded rumors and smears
from actual attempts at subversion. Fabien distinguished them
easily, even if he was predisposed to believe allegations of con-
spiracy and didn't shrink from carrying out dismissals, arrests,
or transfers to the unit specially created as a
gilded limbo for military officers of doubtful reliability: the Co-
ordinating Council for the Defense of the Nation, the CCDN.
Privately, the army brass called it the Correctional Center for
Disgraced Nonentities. Those assigned to it were never again
entrusted with any real responsibility, and they were kept under
tight surveillance.*

*She generally approved of Fabien's decisions. Except when
he went after her personal military escort. Men who were well-
trained, rigorously correct, and closely attentive to her protection and welfare. She was not oblivious to the rampant rumors
about her relationships with two of them. As if every friendship
between a man and a woman had to lead inevitably to a bed.
She had never cared to defend her reputation. Personally, she
preferred to maintain a slyly ambiguous and tantalizing veil*

*over her relationships with these men. Certain memories be-
longed only to those who had lived them. Those officers were
very handsome specimens! Nicely filling out their trim uniforms, conscious of their powers of seduction. They attracted
attention, and several women were jealous of the confidential
rapport she had developed with them. Regarding special tasks
to be accomplished, services rendered, advice provided. So, she
acted diligently and deftly to shield them from Fabien's suspicions. Warned them against all threats, gave them the necessary
resources to shelter themselves and their families, told them
where to take refuge until calm was restored. Before the doubts
were transformed into unshakeable certitudes. Once the Deceased had someone in his sights, it was difficult to divert him
to another prey. She preferred not to abuse her influence. She
reserved it for important occasions, those she deemed fundamental.*

« »

You spent a good part of that last year making allusions to my
boyfriends, or rather to the lack of boyfriends in my life. "Marie-
Ange, I don't hear you talking anymore about that young ac-
countant you met at Madame Désamours's house. And the
customs officer's grandson who used to phone you constantly,
what happened to him?" You knew very well, Maman, that I
didn't keep any boyfriend longer than six months. Contrary to
what I heard you tell a nosey cousin, this was not to avoid making a commitment. No, it's because my heart is frozen between
fear and regret. I run away as soon as I feel the first stirrings of
affection.

I've spent my life trembling in fear of past events, wrestling
with demons that have become mine. How can I fall in love
when I carry this perpetual anxiety within me? And yet I would
like so much to be able to connect with someone and allow the
relationship to impose its own calendar and colors on me—joy-
ous or somber, no matter! To revel in the euphoria of closeness
and let myself be carried like an infinitesimal grain of sand until
I come to rest somewhere or other, happy or unhappy, but excited and alive.

« »

The selection of Fabien Doréval's successor was one of her rare defeats. The worst. Also the most humiliating. For everyone who knew the family, who spent time with the children, followed their development, their involvement in political matters, the choice should have been easy. Marie-Danielle possessed all the necessary qualities to succeed her father: determination, vision, intelligence, and toughness. She never hemmed and hawed at crucial moments. Never succumbed to a soft-heartedness that might have made her look weak. She could anticipate an individual's lapses in order to take advantage of them. She was in her element both times she replaced a bedridden Fabien. Especially the second.

When, after strong persuasion on Odile's part, he finally admitted that the end was inexorably approaching. With a firm hand, their eldest daughter was fulfilling the duties of the presidency, doling out the various tasks, handling calls and correspondence, making decisions without hesitation. Nevertheless, Fabien categorically refused to make her his successor. He tried to answer Odile's reasoning with specious arguments that she easily refuted. In the end, he said to her, "She's only a woman." As if she, too, had to acknowledge the manifest impossibility— as he saw it—of a woman in sole charge of the country.

Her hand refused to take orders from her tired brain. Her weepiness embarrassed her for several reasons. She used to think that only weaklings shed tears over past actions. Cowering behind their regrets. Tears have never resolved anything. She had seen men whimper and squeal when they realized that Fabien, having learned of, surmised, or suspected their treason, had condemned them. That had changed absolutely nothing, as their wailing had debased them still more in the Deceased's estimation. Annoyed, she tried again to brush the tears from her eyes. In vain. None of her fingers moved. How she hated losing control over the body that had submitted to her will throughout her life! The imperious way she held her head, her distinguished bearing, her measured and sparing movements—

all those she had acquired through tenacity and discipline. She had multiplied her genetic capital a hundredfold. To present the lofty image that defined her. These days, however, her fingers and the rest of her body were deserting her. She let out a raspy sound, inhuman to her ears. In an instant, like an unexpected breeze, a fresh towel wiped her eyes. Grateful, she let herself be overcome by silence.

« »

Why a benevolent gesture toward this woman who no doubt participated in the decisions of her dictator husband? She helped send so many people to their deaths, contributed to the destruction of entire families. Yours—ours—came out of it broken. Your brother, my father, all the people whose stories I knew and all the others who lost their lives with no witnesses to keep their memory alive. This pitiful woman on her deathbed, isn't she responsible? I mustn't forget that.

This evening, the widow's shriveled fingers encircled my wrist in a grip astonishingly tight for someone so feeble. In the twinkling of an eye, my gaze met a pair of alert and darting eyes. The celebrated face became animated before me, haughty, inscrutable. Then, an instant later, I saw only the parchmented skin of eyelids once again closed. I heard her breathing even more raucously than usual under the whiteness of the sheet. But the throaty yet distinct utterance left me no retreat. "Thank you." Slowly, the fingers let go, one after another. As if in spite of themselves. I gently withdrew my hand and moved away from the bed.

« »

Marie-Danielle never forgave her father. Wasn't that the reason for her dry eyes and pouty chin at the funeral? Fabien's dogged insistence on ignoring her abilities, relegating her to certain secondary functions because of her gender. Plus his stubborn resolve to banish his son-in-law, Michel Durandique, mainly on the basis of allegations made by his scheming private secretary. Until the last, Fabien failed to understand that the younger generation was much less accepting of discrimina-

tion against women. She had sensed this in the behavior of the
younger nurses and in the attitudes of the secretaries and the
married daughters of her women friends. The wind was chang-
ing, slowly but unmistakably. And so much the better, she felt.

Even so, she had always eyed with considerable distrust the
campaigns and initiatives of the activists from the Women's
League for Social and Community Action. Those ladies who, for
the most part, lived at a safe remove from the real social prob-
lems and who presumed to speak for all Quisqueyan women.
Yes, she had mistrusted those lawyers, pretentious intellectuals,
and idle housewives. Most of the time, the group would criticize
without proposing solutions. The practice of sending children
in from the rural areas to live with relatives in the city and do
domestic chores in return for lodging, board, and school tu-
ition—a tradition that had existed for decades—those women
dared to compare it to slavery. Unable to understand that the
peasant parents were acting for the best, investing in the fu-
ture of their son or daughter. A number of these children had
learned a trade after several years of primary education: sewing,
auto mechanics, cooking, woodworking. Some had even passed
the qualifying exam and earned secondary diplomas.

Fabien was the first to think of enacting laws to protect these
young domestic workers. Of course, the abuses and excesses
could never be totally eradicated, but given the peasantry's de-
privation, the practice has clearly been beneficial. It's wrong
to confuse the aberrations with the norm. Besides, most of the
people who criticize the system also profit from it. A bunch of
hypocrites! The legions of underpaid domestics in the homes of
these crusading women free them up to write their pamphlets
and organize marches for the betterment of women's lives.

« »

I know that you despaired of having grandchildren and that
you left this world with your heart pining for their love. As if
you knew I had closed that door and intended to remain child-
less. You stopped raising the question with me, certain that you
must somehow have reinforced my aversion to motherhood.

Although I did try to embrace the idea of having kids, Maman, anxiety overwhelmed me every time.

Last week I couldn't invent any new excuses to justify a third postponement of my visit to Martine. She's an old college friend who just had a baby. But first I went with two girlfriends to a baby store and impulsively chose a gift. A chubby stuffed animal with a huge green and yellow bow. Both in the Metro and on the street, I felt incredibly awkward, as if I were heading for my execution with the hangman's noose over my arm.

When I arrived at Martine's, it was even worse. I had to listen to the others rhapsodize. "How handsome he is! Oh! He has your eyes. Look at his tiny hands." Motionless and mute, feigning the sudden onset of a cold, I stared across the room at the infant. The odor of mother's milk, blended with the fragrance of sweet and delicate toiletries, reached my nostrils, and I wanted to let myself be swallowed up by it. I would have liked so much to hug the little body to me, as the others had done, and squeeze it until my tears flowed. Powerless to move, I pasted a tense smile on my lips, nodding from time to time in response to others' comments. I eventually slipped away with the promise to return as soon as I'd shaken off this untimely cold. Then, on the way down the stairs, distraught and gasping, I burst into drawn-out sobs. With my arms dangling ridiculously from my body.

I'm so afraid of having a child and spoiling its life, turning it into a creature like me, with fear dogging its heels.

« »

How she scorned women who shrank behind their husbands, women who saw their charge as solely to obey, stay in the shadows, and not stir up discord in the marital domain. She had always bluntly expressed her opinions, even when they didn't coincide with the Deceased's. They often argued out of sight of prying eyes, since she didn't want in any way to create the image of a troubled couple. But sometimes, like the time she had wanted to defend her daughter and her grandsons, she had no longer cared about decorum. On that day he had dared to com-

*mit an unpardonable act! Yes, she finally had to admit it to her-
self. Her resentment toward the Deceased for that slap, those
furious and deranged eyes, still festered. The arm poised to land
a second blow as their son was rushing to restrain it. She had
not forgiven him for that. Kept to herself, also, the nauseating
sense of frustration brought on by Fabien's unilateral decisions
and by his colleagues' attitudes verging on condescension. Until
they learned to their detriment exactly who they were dealing
with. She knew how to take revenge without fretting over it,
striking hard and accurately.*

*Her daughters had inherited her independence of mind. The
second a little less so than the others, with her tendency to hide
behind a man, both in public and in private. Odile never trusted
any man completely. In her days as a nurse in the maternity
ward at Bon Séjour, she had witnessed instructive examples of
the shamelessness of some men. Of course, her personal experience had relieved her of all naïveté on that score, but she was
nonetheless disgusted time and again by the cynicism of the
new fathers. Many greeted the newborn with doubt and skepticism. With remarks like, "Am I really the father?" and, "That
baby doesn't even look like me!" Sometimes the man's mother
would show up to examine the baby, palpate him, look for a
sign, a birthmark associated with the family down through the
generations, a splayed toe, asymmetric lips. And implacably,
the verdict would fall, a negative scowl, a shake of the head.
The man would reject all responsibility for the baby. Without
any right of appeal.*

*One day the family of an alleged father turned up at the
clinic with some blood. It was the man's blood, and they demanded that it be force-fed to the baby. If he got sick, that
would be irrefutable proof he wasn't really the man's offspring.
The nurse, mother, and wife in her was so outraged that she
lost her usual calm and forcibly ejected the representatives of
the father's family from the maternity ward. Threatening to call
the police if they dared to come near the baby.*

*The widow winced as she thought of this incident. The staff
in the maternity unit talked about it for quite some time. Di-
vided into two groups: on the one hand, those who were of-*

fended by the fathers' attitudes; on the other, those who tried
to justify them, casting doubt on the veracity of the mothers'
claims.

Life had thus proven to her that a woman owed it to herself
to be independent, even if she didn't subscribe to the inflamma-
tory speeches of the feminists from the League. She brought up
her children, both daughters and son, to respect themselves. She
imparted to them some basic principles: think independently,
behave with dignity, don't let anyone step on your toes. Take
care of your appearance. Watch your back. Protect the family
to the end.

And yet today she was dying alone.

<< >>

I think it's time for me to say good-bye to the ghosts. To the
biggest absence in my life, the one who takes up the most space,
for you have never wanted to explain the circumstances of his
death.

Today I'm ready to reconstruct the disastrous day you always kept to yourself, just as you never mentioned your six
years of marriage, as if sharing it with me would have abridged
or changed that carefree interlude. In trying to picture the two
of you as a happy couple, I must rely on my imagination to fill
the gaps and blank spots in my frustratingly scant memories.
To place in the domestic scene the little girl who was me on that
November day. The happiness was truly present, even though
it stemmed in part from suffering. And it was capable of holding us in the warmth of our day-to-day routine. The gales of
laughter, the passionate embraces, the flights of tenderness, the
words of endearment when you both left the house in the morning, the kiss of greeting when you reunited. "See you later."
"Have a good day." "Take care of yourself." "I love you." That
last day, what did you say to each other before leaving home,
each in your own direction? You on the way to drop me off at
preschool, before going on to a job interview. My father bound
for the high school where he taught history, before proceeding
to the radio station to record his broadcast. Surely you kissed
on that November morning. Did Papa give me a hug before

catching a taxi that would get him to school on time? Did he squeeze me really tight? Was he struck by a premonition that this would be the last time he saw his wife and child? I see him now, Maman, kneeling in front of me, and I snuggle against him as his arms encircle my shoulders. I inhale the freshness of a green shirt against my skin. The scent a powerful blend of chalk, aftershave, and books. A voice never erased from my memory: "Have a good day, my little angel." I fill myself with love, Maman, and then, because there's no choice, I let my father go.

I can unhesitatingly situate the day within its context. It's so easy for me to dive into this universe, though it's been more than twenty years; I find myself back in it, but with the eyes of an adult. In that fateful year, under the reign of Jean-Paul Doréval and his mother—sometimes called a modern-day Cornelia* by her admirers—an independent press came to life. The year 1980 marked the coalescence of dissenting voices. At first tangled up in its promises of liberalization and intent on staying in power, the government was ultimately forced to react to every criticism of the regime. Intellectuals, artists, and writers were seething. Petitions were circulating. Theatrical productions dramatizing the reign of terror during Fabien's regime—and Jean-Paul's mitigated version of the same—were being performed pretty much everywhere. The government decided to put on a show of force. Some said the widow played a pivotal role in that decision, but who knows? Jean-Paul Doréval launched a crackdown worthy of his father. An infamous Friday. The tiger cub bared his claws. The forces of order rounded up journalists, writers, artists. Locked them up, tortured the unlucky ones, allowed some to take refuge in foreign embassies, murdered others who had even worse luck than the torture victims. A witness recounted how some journalists tried to escape. Three units of the new elite presidential bodyguard, the Panthers, were waiting for them at the street corner. The men in their camouflage suits opened fire. The civilians crumpled to the ground, wounded or dead.

My father was among the latter. With other anonymous fatalities whose names are hardly ever mentioned nowadays. He had just begun working as a commentator on a radio station in Port-du-Roi. In addition to his work as a social studies teacher at two secondary schools in the capital. To help make ends meet. To give us something better—me, his daughter barely past her fifth birthday, and you, his wife, who had just finished a management course and begun job hunting. Also to act, to speak out. Not just to stand there with his arms crossed and his mouth stopped up. He envisioned a serious and dynamic commentary about various fields of work, a broadcast capable of evoking an enthusiastic reception, of examining the business elite and their complicity with officials at the Ministry of Social Affairs, of exposing the pressures brought to bear on the labor unions.

Papa didn't return home that evening. With the help of friends, you searched for him in all the places where the regime might have taken him. The police headquarters, Fort Décembre, the general hospital, even the private hospitals just in case he might have ended up there. Then, as a last resort, the morgue, with a chill in your heart. It's there that you found him. With two bullet holes in his blood-soaked green shirt. One in the small of his back, the other at the back of his neck.

« »

She was leaving with the certitude that the family constituted the focal point of an individual's personality: the nucleus of frustrations and drives, the source of life's possibilities. Even if, as is obviously the case, experiences external to the family setting influenced the mature personality. Even now, when she found herself too often alone, in this nursing home reeking with the stench of worn-out bodies, she still believed it. Family members certainly came to visit her. First of all, her sisters, who were still living. Clara never came, but the other two did. Angela, flying in from Florida with stories of her offspring settled in Quisqueya and grappling with the complications of a daily existence in perpetual turmoil. Emma, who had emigrated to Panama City long before the exile, with her growing retail business, two new locations this year, the children and grandchil-

*dren likewise multiplying, three more of the latter, now num-
bering five. Emma's brood sometimes came along to keep her
company. Also Odile's own children. With the beginnings of a
farewell in their expressions. Sincere but hurried. Touched to
see her but soon ill-at-ease.*

*Signs of financial strain were everywhere in this suburban
Parisian nursing home. The tattered curtains, the scuffed fur-
nishings, the drab, unpolished floors, and the resigned faces of
the staff. Odile's children were accustomed to the luxury earned
by her exertions. These children whose parents and grandparents had lived through childhood with uncertain mornings, evenings with empty bellies, and nights with hunger-fueled dreams.
They wriggled with embarrassment when they saw the nursing
home's modest decor. Bit their lips, observed the surroundings
with an air of annoyance, or stared at the wall as if the story of
their lives were written there. In the end, she stopped looking at
them and closed her eyes in their presence. Spoke to them less
and less, without determining whether her fatigue was weighing her down to that extent or whether the desire to hear herself
talk had fled. Bringing her closer to the day when she would
lapse into total silence.*

<< >>

Don't be angry with me, Maman, if I switch off your storytelling today and repress your memories. I've had enough of letting
myself be submerged by the words of others. Your voice, your
mother's, Jean-Édouard's, Papa's, and the voices of all the other
characters in your innumerable stories that have been heaped
on top of my own story for my entire life.

You, Maman, so attached to your family, you for whom the
mere mention of your brother put flecks of rainbow in your
eyes, why didn't you think of giving me a brother, or a little
sister? Someone with whom I would have stored up so many
memories, both trivial and profound, that our existences would
have blended forever, like a vast mosaic with unexpected colors,
riotous or soothing, but always overflowing with life. Together,
we would have exchanged so many touching anecdotes, such
an ebb and flow of searing anger and tender smiles that even

our quarrels would have had the zest of friendship. Maman, you drew strength from your memories of star-strewn nights, of delicately crafted tenderness, of laughter and *lagos** in the midst of the dictatorship, but still you piled misery on me. You were occasionally empathetic, but always solitary. Blinded by the harsh radiance of your pain and rage, I could perceive only faint glimmers of your joy.

Today I would like to build myself spaces that are both diverse and roomy, intimate and welcoming, where suffering and elation coexist, where both memories and possibilities would find room to live. I would like to stay up at night, for the simple pleasure of passing the night free from alarming dreams. To stay alert in the expectation of daybreak. For the ineffable joy of its first glow. Precious. Unique. In unspoken collusion with the dazzling brightness to come.

« »

April 1981. Another ceremony, but this time the Deceased was not present at her side. She was the principal figure. In her capacity as widow of the greatest leader of the Dorévalist revolution, the national legislature was awarding her the official title of Guardian of the Revolution. Her widow's status finally guaranteed her exclusive honors. Though often decried, a solitary existence could be highly beneficial and sometimes indispensable. After her colossal grief, she had appreciated those moments of calm, of intimate encounter, without pretense and with no pressure to explain anything at all for reasons of love or duty.

Guardian of the Revolution. She richly deserved the title. Having battled after Fabien's death to prevent the country from sliding into chaos. Fortunately, she was surrounded by solid people she could count on. The "dinosaurs." She was aware of that disparagingly sarcastic nickname given to the authentic and faithful protectors of the Dorévalist ideals. Moreover, she suspected that the Foreigner had coined the name to advance the campaign she was leading against Odile in the palace. Where Odile had lived for at least a third of her life. One day, in a fit of anger, she left, taking her keys—that's the truth. Why wouldn't she? That odious woman, her face taut with hatred and ambition, was employing Odile's only son against her and against the country. Sabotaging her initiatives. Wasting the taxpayers' money, flouncing around in front of everyone, and shamelessly enriching her friends and relatives, all of them clueless elitists like herself.

If Odile had not managed to keep her wits and exert influence over her son's decisions, Jean-Paul's government would not have lasted as long as it did. Lambert's presence at his side helped him withstand the pressure from all quarters and display the necessary firmness. "Economic revolution," intoned her son, without really understanding, especially at the beginning, that a firm hand was still necessary. Letting people express their disagreement, their grievances, gave them the idea that in due course some of their demands could be met and their most pressing requests dealt with. Democracy cannot succeed without a tangible improvement in living conditions. The little priest experienced that just recently. He was compelled to take drastic measures to muzzle the opposition's rabble-rousing rhetoric. Once in power, all those who believed that it was easy to rule came to recognize the complexity of the task. Jean-Paul, too, had to do an about-face and return to the good old methods. Some have said he blundered in ordering the arrests and other authoritarian measures of November 1980, but the steps he took were necessary. The government had to clamp down in order to avoid anarchy.

No, there was no bungling on that morning of November 1980. The revolutionary regime was showing its might.

« »

Are we prisoners of our memory, or is memory instead beholden to our weaknesses and hidden wounds? Can our memories still flow freely when our scars accumulate and surround them like a gory ring of barbed wire? My memory is freeing itself today and bringing me a spontaneous recollection like a serendipitous magical charm.

It's a summer's day at Descailles, and I catch sight of an elusive and captivating image. Man Nini is making paper dolls and gluing them together to form a chain. Still alert, she is eager to kindle sparks of delight in her great-granddaughter's eyes. She used to call me "Tizanj." How had I forgotten her voice? With a few deft movements, despite her arthritic fingers, Man Nini would cut out a line of little female figures with pliable bodies and grinning faces. She'd hand them over to me with a back-and-forth motion of her slack-skinned arm, and for me they were the most marvelous gift. I, in turn, would make them twirl as I danced around with them. A whole string of dolls in colors that varied according to the paper used to make each one. A long chain of little silhouettes, bathed with sunlight and dancing in the wind, fragile and beautiful.

« »

How tired her mind suddenly felt! She would like very much to rest, to stop thinking about things—but not to die. To float in a lethargic state that would bring serenity and peace, without losing the ability to emerge from it from time to time. To sift through the past once again, organize her ideas, rid herself of emotions too strong to allow her to fall asleep without a last look.

A foreign journalist, bolder than the others, had one day asked her a question before Fabien could intervene from his adjacent chair and abruptly terminate the interview. "Madame Doréval, as a woman and as a nurse by profession, how do you feel when confronted with accusations of torture launched from overseas against your husband's government?" In no way had the question haunted her, despite what some might think. To preserve the gains of the revolution, the Deceased had been obliged to act in a manner that was sometimes brutal. Their enemies bore a much heavier responsibility for the retaliation provoked by their intemperate, ill-considered, and egotistical actions. Also, the critics exaggerated the casualty figures. To claim an average of more than one hundred killings per day! What a grotesque exaggeration!

And they were never inclined to acknowledge the regime's achievements. For example, the Fabien Doréval International Airport, built under difficult conditions. Since her family

*had left, the unlucky airport has seen its name changed, like
a weathervane, at the whim of successive governments, none
of them capable of staying in power. The Avenue Desravines,
paved with four and a half miles of concrete that have survived
the negligent installation of the sewers, the incomplete disposal
of surplus materials, and more than thirty years of heavy use
by truckers. A modern building to house the offices of the tax
administration and likewise for the police headquarters. And
to be sure, the housing development that once bore her name!*

*The journalist's question didn't prey on her mind, but it
sometimes surprised her by recurring in her thoughts. She
was still sure of the response, yet the backdrop was becoming
murkier. New objects were looming up unexpectedly. Severed
hands, gouged-out eyes. A shape noticed at the turning of a
corridor. A pair of lips glimpsed at the door to the little back
room where the Deceased would personally direct the interro-
gations. A profile immobilized between two uniformed guards.
The shock of recognition of an old friend from the orphanage.
A shudder. The refusal to believe it. And unwelcome flashbacks
like a leaden lump in the depths of her memory. Her name was
Henriette. A pudgy girl with thick red hair, whose good humor seemed to defy her bad luck and succeeded in penetrating
the young Odile's cynical aloofness. "Who was that?" she later
asked Fabien. "An opponent's wife. We finally got her to talk.
She was in league with him." "Where did they take her?" "To
Fort Décembre." It probably wasn't her. Henriette wouldn't
get involved in political matters. Maybe her husband; after all,
Odile didn't know the man! Henriette would have immediately
revealed everything she knew. If she did know something, Henriette wouldn't expose herself to torture like that. She wouldn't
let herself be taken to Fort Décembre. Henriette knew that
people who went in there seldom came out. And if they did,
in what condition! No, that woman couldn't be her old friend
from the orphanage. Odile crammed the image back into her
tormented memory, where it would patiently await its next turn
to resurface.*

« »

I want to live. Without the oppressive burden that I've inherited. Without fears or anxieties except those that life will bring me in its ordinary course.

« »

Unconsciously, she was slipping toward oblivion. The strident noises of the oxygen regulator and the other machines did not awaken her. Suddenly, cool hands grasped her, shook her, brought her back to the world. A puff of air invaded her constricted lungs. Borne toward the oxygen like a drowning person, she opened her mouth wide and gasped for air. Reflexive vanity made her want to close it, but she couldn't. Strange, rude, and barbarous croaks were escaping from someone's throat—her own. The needle and the intravenous tube were encumbering her, and she tried vainly to remove them. Let out a scream of impotence and rage. Struggled. "Calm down! The doctor is on his way. I sent someone to find him." The voice was speaking their shared language. She let the familiar inflections descend drop by drop to calm her anxiety. The oxygen mask enfolded her within its tepid silence, and for a brief moment her eyes opened onto the face that was leaning over her, before her eyelids dropped again.

« »

While the medical team is attending to the dictator's widow, I notice several staff members staring perplexedly at me. No doubt my face reflects my disarray.

Why, then, had I given the alarm? I who had wanted, for the repose of my memory, to see this old woman die by my own hands, and here I have just saved her life. And what a life! An unrelievedly dull existence, with the colors of faded white sheets and sterilized walls, and with food that is predigested to the point of squeezing out all taste and aroma. An existence on the borderland of death.

I followed my instincts, Maman, just as you would undoubtedly have done. Despite your long stay in a maze of dread, you instilled in me a profound respect for life. The reverential attitude you took on quite naturally when contemplating a baby's

smile or swelling waves. The atavistic resistance to death. All
the emotions that had overwhelmed me when you closed your
eyes forever in my presence. One moment alive, albeit declining, and then suddenly nothingness. The doctors and all their
modern technology couldn't save you. You had departed irretrievably. In contrast, the old woman is little by little resuming
her slow-motion existence. Apparently as listless as before, or
even more so, yet still alive. I could have let her die. Easily. By
doing nothing. By saying nothing. But you know very well, Maman, you had always known, that I could never have done that.
There have already been too many deaths around me.

Besides my father, how many others had perished? Anonymous, forgotten as the years go by. Perhaps still mourned by
the tears of a close relative, but unnoticeable among all the
other victims of the dictatorship. No remarkable story accompanying their death. No instructive anecdote, like that of the
restaurant owner who, through ignorance, inattentiveness, or
bravery—it doesn't matter—served a meal to members of the
insurgent group, the Thirteen, before their entry into the capital. He passed into history as a victim of the Doréval dictatorship because he sold a plateful of rice. Executed for so trivial an
act! Gone to his death like so many others. For most of them,
no heroic story like that of the militant who took his own life
when Fabien Doréval's forces surrounded the cave at Fancy,
where he had taken refuge. Faced with his refusal to surrender, they had dragged his mother to the scene to use her as a
hostage, either as bait or as a human shield. The militant killed
himself. History, as if by chance, does not record what became
of the mother. Apart from the ordeal of watching helplessly as
the militia unit attacked her son, of hearing him shoot himself
several yards away from her, what was her fate? Vexed at not
being able to capture an enemy alive, incensed by the public
humiliation this militant had inflicted on them, what did they
do to his mother?

So many stories of extraordinary men and women! The
young mother not yet thirty, arrested at the same time as her
two brothers and killed at Fort Décembre. The celebrated
writer tortured for months because of his leftist ideas. The

child mowed down by one of the many vehicles in the young president's reckless, rowdy motorcade. The families of victims forever maimed, retaining in their imaginations the body parts torn away or mutilated.

So many overlooked stories of men and women just guilty of having been alive at the wrong moment, in the wrong place. So many people executed in humdrum fashion. With all of their potential. Crushed, annihilated. As if their existences represented nothing but stray marks to be wiped from the blackboard. So many stories linked to one another by the ordinariness of the event or by the symbolism of the gesture. Or, more simply, by the human possibilities laid waste. My father, my uncle, the resister whose grandchildren will never know him, Madame So-and-So's husband, the grocer's cousin, his friend's godfather, the mother of the little girl who will not be born, the boy who should have been born. All those men, women, and children who could have been happy. For a little longer.

everyone lives the same

Once more I approach the bed. The widow's breathing is stronger and stronger. Outside, the December cold is coating the windows with frost. The room seems to shrink, isolating us from all outside intrusions. Keeping the past and the ghosts at bay. Crowding out regrets and reproaches. Leaving nothing but the intoxicating scent of salt air and the tantalizing image of a chain of little paper figures dancing in the sunshine.

Sitting very close to the emaciated body, I wait.

keeping her in her guilt and pain

GLOSSARY

bateyes: Squalid sheds used to house agricultural workers, the vast majority of them undocumented Haitian immigrants, in the sugar plantations of the Dominican Republic.

carreau de terre: Approximately 3.19 acres.

Cité Ochan: An invented name (from the Creole word for "Cheers!") for Cité Soleil. The latter is the current name of the residential area originally named for François Duvalier's wife. (Trans.)

Cornelia: Cornelia Africana, mother of the Gracchi, two high-minded tribunes of the Roman Republic. She is often held up as the foremost example of the virtuous Roman woman. (Trans.)

good luck baths: Ritual baths taken by practitioners of Haitian Vodou to enlist the protection of the *loas.* (Trans.)

jetedlo: A ritual whereby the Vodou follower throws three drops of liquid on the ground by way of greeting and invitation to the ancestral and family spirits. Depending on the rite, the liquid may be water, rum, wine, or coffee.

lago: A game akin to hide-and-seek.

little priest: The activist cleric and politician Jean-Bertrand Aristide. An outspoken critic of Duvalierism, he served as president of Haiti during three separate periods between 1991 and 2004. He left the priesthood in 1994. (Trans.)

loas: Spirits of the Haitian Vodou pantheon grouped into families or clans to form the nations observing the Rada, Petro, or Congo rites.

mambo: A Vodou priestess at the head of a congregation with the same authority and attributes as her male counterpart, the *ougan.*

mini-jazz: A form of jazz with indigenous Haitian roots, as well as influences from rock music. The style came to prominence in Haiti in the 1960s. The term also refers to any of the small bands that played the music. (Trans.)

ougan: A Vodou priest who conducts ceremonies and serves as an intermediary between the *loas* and the faithful.

poteau mitan: The central post of the peristyle, the Vodou place of worship. The *poteau* serves as a conduit to the spirits.

PPPL: The Parti populaire pour la libération, a left-wing movement ruthlessly repressed by François Duvalier. (Trans.)

Radio Ochan: An invented adaptation of "Radio Soleil," a broadcast outlet founded by the Catholic Church in 1978. The station was a beacon of opposition to "Baby Doc" Duvalier's regime. (Trans.)

rara: A festive group of peasants who parade along rural roads and lanes, and at times in urban areas, singing and dancing to the rousing rhythm of drums and bamboo horns (*vaccins*) during the Lenten period.

Tonton Macoutes: The nickname for the Voluntaires de la sécurité nationale (VSN), a dreaded militia force under the Duvalier regimes. "Tonton Macoute" means "Uncle Gunnysack," and it referred originally to a mythical bogeyman who kidnapped misbehaving children and stuffed them into his sack.

vèvè: A drawing traced on the ground with ash, wheat flour, or cornmeal, depicting the symbol that corresponds to a particular *loa*.

VSN: See Tonton Macoutes.

zombification: The supposed reanimation of a corpse. Reported instances of zombie-like behavior probably result from sublethal poisonings of live victims. Still, the belief in reanimation is persistent enough that an attempt to steal the dictator's body for such a purpose could not be ruled out. (Trans.)

Zoreille: A term commonly used in the French Antilles to denote a person from mainland France who has come to live in the Antilles. The term has a parallel meaning elsewhere in the French Overseas Departments and Territories. (Trans.)

AFTERWORD

Jason Herbeck

When, after twenty-five years in exile, Jean-Claude "Baby Doc" Duvalier unexpectedly returned to Haiti on January 16, 2011, the polarized yet strikingly muted public response was in some ways eerily reminiscent of public reaction during the decades-long era of repression in which he and his father, François "Papa Doc" Duvalier, ruled Haiti (1957–86). While hundreds of Haitians took to the streets in a "carnival-like atmosphere"[1] to cheer the arrival of Baby Doc in Port-au-Prince, the apprehension of a large swath of Haiti's population was, surprisingly, by and large indiscernible. In fact, Duvalier's "unbelievable" reappearance on the Haitian scene resulted in remarkably few manifestations of outright public protest,[2] and, in the days following his return, many of those who did speak out attributed his arrival in Haiti to a shrewd political maneuver on the part of outgoing President René Préval, who, it was suggested, wanted to divert attention from a highly critical report delivered only days earlier by the Joint Organization of American States–Caribbean Community Electoral Observation Mission.[3] Such theories have remained speculative at best. However, the failure of the Préval administration to take an immediate stance on Duvalier's homecoming is nonetheless surprising given Préval's public statement in 2007 that Duvalier would face charges of political tyranny, corruption, and crimes against humanity should he choose to return.

While a handful of Haitian organizations such as the National Human Rights Defense Network (RNDDH) immediately denounced Duvalier's return and demanded that he be brought to justice for his past crimes,[4] the prevailing response in Haiti was described as one of stupefaction and "deafening silence."[5] In what clearly amounts to an understatement, Lemoine Bonneau, a journalist for *Le Nouvelliste*, noted the day after Duvalier's return, "If this visit elates the Duvalierists who dream of a time past, it also constitutes for certain victims of the dictatorship an immense disappointment."[6] Perhaps most telling of the disquiet with which many Haitians reacted to Duvalier *fils*'s homecoming is that only five of the estimated tens of thousands of people allegedly detained and tortured during the dictator's fifteen-year rule formally brought personal charges against him in the months following his arrival at the Toussaint Louverture International Airport in the nation's capital.[7]

In terms of immediate response, the international community proved by far the most critical and vehement about Jean-Claude Duvalier's return. Human Rights Watch, Amnesty International, and other humanitarian organizations from around the world urged President Préval's administration to take swift action in charging Duvalier with a long list of crimes he and his secret paramilitary police, the Tonton Macoutes, had allegedly committed during his brutal fifteen-year reign.

In the days following Jean-Claude Duvalier's return, the Haitian government eventually introduced charges, including corruption and embezzlement (the ousted dictator is believed to have fled the country with an estimated $300 million belonging to the Haitian people). However, Duvalier was soon afterward released from custody, and a court order placing him under house arrest on March 24, 2011, was criticized as pro forma when—in clear defiance of the warrant—Duvalier was seen driving around Port-au-Prince and dining at upscale restaurants in neighboring Pétionville.[8]

The ambivalent state of affairs surrounding the former dictator has hardly become more transparent under the current administration of President Michel Joseph Martelly (2011–present). Curiously, Martelly's stance on both Duvalier and the former president Jean-Bertrand Aristide (who, coincidentally, returned from exile to Haiti two months after Duvalier, on March 18, 2011)[9] appears to have come nearly full circle since Martelly's presidential election campaign, when he suggested that both men be granted amnesty. Although Martelly soon afterward retracted the statement, expressing his deference to the court system, his government—in seeming contradiction to the court-ordered house arrest—renewed Duvalier's diplomatic passport under the pretense that he was entitled to it as a former head of state. Similarly, the official invitation Martelly extended to Duvalier and Matthieu Prosper Avril[10] to attend the January 1, 2014, ceremony in Gonaïves in commemoration of the 210th anniversary of the country's independence was decried as both "an unspeakable insult to the nation" and "an affront to the memory of thousands of victims of the Duvalierist dictatorship."[11] When questioned about the implications of impunity that the invitation might convey, a spokesperson for Martelly insisted that the decision be understood as a "call for unity."

On February 28, 2013, more than two years after his return to Haitian soil, Jean-Claude Duvalier appeared in court for the first time to face charges of corruption and human rights violations. During the five-hour-long hearing, he unequivocally denied any wrongdoing in relation to alleged crimes ranging from embezzlement, misappropriation of funds, and theft to repression, torture, and political assassinations. Furthermore, when asked if he had fully assumed his responsibilities as head of state from 1971 to 1986, a clearly indignant Duvalier became in turn accusatory: "I did as much as I could as the person responsible for assuring a better way of life to my fellow countryman. However, at the time, my government was dealing effectively with poverty. During that period, all State businesses were making money [and] parents could afford to send their children to school. I'm not saying life was ideal, but the people could at least live decently. . . . I have come back to a ruined country [and] limitless corruption that impedes development. . . . And so in returning, I can ask, 'What have you done with my country?'"[12] Although the picture the ousted dictator paints of Haiti in the 1970s and early 1980s is arguably rosier than many might remember it, it is nevertheless true that under Duvalierism the Haitian population's basic sanitary, educational, and economic needs were met with much greater consistency than when he returned in 2011. Even making allowance for political instability, UN embargos, devastating tropical storms, a mass rural exodus to urban areas, and the 2010 earthquake and subsequent cholera outbreak, Haiti's infrastructure and overall quality of life have significantly deteriorated since Duvalier relinquished power. Furthermore, because upward of 60 percent of the population is under the age of twenty-five, the vast majority of Haitians have no personal memory with which to look back—critically or otherwise—upon Duvalierist rule. Consequently, as William Booth states, "Although an older generation in Haiti recalls with a shudder the bad things that happened in the Duvalier years, many Haitians are nostalgic for the era, when the country was more prosperous, tourists were not afraid to come and Haiti was the world's leading maker of baseballs."[13]

Regardless of the conflicting degrees of interest, horror, and skepticism with which generations of Haitians view the return of Baby Doc to Haiti and the urgency of bringing him to trial, the attention of the Haitian population as a whole can only be sustained for so long.[14] Given the more pressing, immediate concerns of day-to-day survival, dwelling too long on the past means turnings one's thoughts from the present and immediate future—something that for many constitutes an ill-afforded luxury.

Nonetheless, as the return of Jean-Claude Duvalier demonstrates, the shadows of the Duvalier era have clearly not receded for good and continue to throw a dark veil on the country today, contributing unmistakably to the complex panorama of present-day preoccupations. As the journalist Danièle Magloire wrote in 2013, on the eve of the fifty-year anniversary of the April 26, 1963, roundup and massacre of more than seventy presumed opponents of François Duvalier, "We will not forget what the Duvalierist dictatorship was!"[15] Refusing to forget, however, presents a double-edged sword. Among the first five individuals to come forward to press personal charges against Duvalier *fils*, Robert Duval—a soccer coach who spent nearly eighteen months in the notorious political prison of Fort Dimanche instituted by Duvalier *père*—expressed little surprise at the relative dearth of plaintiffs: "That's the strength of the stigma that Duvalier left on this country. He may not have been on our minds, but now that he's back, we see that the fear of him is still in our hearts."[16]

François Duvalier

Although François Duvalier's (1907–1971) nickname "Papa Doc" came to signify repression and violence during his reign as dictator, evoking in many a sense of dread, the sobriquet was initially bestowed upon him affectionately in reference to the discipline to which he devoted himself from a young age. Having graduated from the University of Haiti School of Medicine in 1934, the Port-au-Prince-born son of a middle-class immigrant family from Martinique (his father was a teacher and magistrate, his mother a baker) rose swiftly through the ranks of the profession. While working as a hospital staff physician in 1939, Duvalier married a nurse, Simone Ovide, with whom he would have four children: Marie Denise, Nicole, Simone, and Jean-Claude. In 1943, Duvalier's interest in combatting the spread of tropical diseases led to his becoming active in an anti-yaws campaign sponsored by the US Army Medical Corps. After studying briefly at the University of Michigan in Ann Arbor in 1944–45, he returned to Haiti, where he quickly ascended under President Dumarsais Estimé to become director general of the National Public Health Service in 1946 and deputy minister of labor in 1948 before being appointed to the post of minister of public health and labor in 1950.

Duvalier remained supportive of Estimé despite the president's dwindling credibility following an unsuccessful attempt to modify the constitution as a means of pursuing a second consecutive term as president. Consequently, when Duvalier openly disapproved of the military coup organized by Paul E. Magloire that forced Estimé into exile in 1950, he left his government post and returned to practicing medicine. Rejoining the American Sanitary Mission in 1951, he used his connections in rural communities in which he worked to organize a grassroots movement in opposition to newly elected President Magloire and, in 1954, was himself forced into hiding as his notoriety in the resistance became more pronounced. When Magloire announced a general amnesty for political opponents in 1956, Duvalier resurfaced and declared his candidacy for president.

During a particularly unstable political period even according to Haitian standards, Duvalier's influence further increased over the subsequent ten months, thanks in part to supporters who played an active role in many of the six governments that came into existence at that time. As a candidate for the upcoming election, Duvalier, who as a child had personally experienced the racial polarization and conflicts spurred by the American occupation of Haiti in 1915–34, appealed to the country's large black majority with a populist, *noiriste* (black nationalism) campaign. As a cofounder of the Griot movement of the 1930s and author of a book on Vodou, Duvalier was "an astute observer of Haitian life and a student of his country's history," and he thus aligned himself with spiritual elements of Haitian culture as a way of expanding his following. Having won over the army and negotiated deals with other presidential candidates, he readily defeated his main opponent, Louis Déjoie, a member of the mulatto elite, on September 22, 1957.

The start of François Duvalier's presidency was anything but smooth, however. In an attempt to consolidate power as quickly as possible, Duvalier effectively banned all opposition parties—as well as, more generally, public or private gatherings of any sort, including film clubs, reading groups, and so forth—and demanded that Parliament allow him to govern by decree. After an attempted military coup failed to oust him from power in July 1958, Papa Doc decided to reduce the army—which he now considered a threat—and, in 1959, created a private paramilitary group called the Volunteers for National Security (Volontaires de la sécurité nationale, or VSN) as a means of suppressing alleged foes of the regime. Better known as the Tonton Macoutes, these "bogeymen," many of whom were not necessarily salaried and thus stole from the people they were ordered to abduct, torture, and kill, readily resorted to intimidation tactics to force the Haitian population into subservience. In April 1961, Duvalier dissolved Parliament, eventually proclaiming himself "president for life" in 1964.

The considerable resources Haiti received from the US government in the form of aid grants during the early years of Duvalier's presidency began to dry up. The increasingly evident modus operandi of coercion and violence behind Duvalier's rule, coupled with his unwillingness to follow the United States' strict accounting procedures as a precondition for continued aid, soon outweighed the benefits of the Haitian president's anti-Communist sentiment along with Haiti's strategic position relative to Cuba, which had initially helped secure US economic support. President John F. Kennedy's administration eventually suspended all aid in mid-1962. Shortly afterward, in 1963, tensions rose drastically between Haiti and neighboring Dominican Republic, which increasingly provided support and asylum to Haitian exiles opposed to the Duvalier regime.

Duvalier remained a formidable dictator up until his death in 1971. During his tenure, Haiti's per-capita income remained the hemisphere's lowest, at less than $75.[18] Able to fend off challenges from both within Haiti and abroad, Duvalier successfully managed a deadly campaign of terror throughout his time in power, which did not end before he had once again modified the Haitian constitution in order to designate his only son, Jean-Claude "Baby Doc" Duvalier, as his successor.

As feared as Papa Doc, Baby Doc, and their Tonton Macoutes were during their nearly three decades in power, the suppressive institution of Duvalierism was not maintained solely on terror, massacres, and the systematic theft of state and personal possessions. As noted by Haïti lutte contre l'impunité (Haiti fights against impunity), "it was also obscurantism in the fullest sense of the word—the type that no government could have imagined as a means of perpetuating its power. Duvalierist terror impregnated the Church [and] religions (Catholicism, Protestantism, Vodou), and colonized the collective imagination."[19] In 1964, Duvalier, in claiming he was the living incarnation of legendary Haitian revolutionaries such as Jean-Jacques Dessalines, Toussaint Louverture, and Alexandre Pétion, presented himself as "the supreme commander of the revolution," "the biggest patriot of all time," and "the champion of national dignity."[20] The Lord's Prayer was rewritten with François Duvalier substituted in place of the Father, or God. Duvalier's uses of Vodou as a way of extending his control and influence were multifold, and increased throughout his presidency. Pretending to be an *ougan,* or Vodou priest, he would often dress like the Vodou divinity Baron Samedi (with a black suit, dark sunglasses, and top hat), affecting a staring gaze and whispered, heavily nasalized speech. Upon falling seriously ill in 1971 (he suffered from prostate cancer, diabetes, and heart trouble), Duvalier summoned a Vodou priest to the presidential palace to hold a ceremony.

To suggest that fear and trepidation were ubiquitous during the Duvalier era is by no means an overstatement. In addition to his own carefully crafted public image, Duvalier's foreboding presence manifested itself physically in the form of the Tonton Macoutes militia and the Fort Dimanche torturer Madame Max Adolphe,[21] as well as emotionally, as a more abstract yet no less ominously perceived threat that ingrained itself at the very heart of the Haitian psyche. Edwidge Danticat, who begins her book *Create Dangerously* with a detailed account of the 1964 public execution of the dissident group Jeune Haïti (Young Haiti, also known as "Les Treize," or "The Thirteen") members Marcel Numa and Louis Drouin, explains how, in the context of this era of suspicion, literature that in appearance had nothing to do with Duvalier's reign could be perceived as highly subversive. Consequently, as evidenced by the clandestine readings of Albert Camus's play *Caligula,* literary works could not only serve as a means of resistance but could be punishable by death: "[B]ooks that might seem innocent . . . could easily betray [those who had them in their possession]. Novels with the wrong titles. Treatises with the right titles and intentions. Strings of words that, uttered, written, or read, could cause a person's death" (9).[22]

It is estimated that up to a million Haitians fled into exile as a result of the systematic human rights violations during the thirty years François and Jean-Claude Duvalier held power[23]— either because of the repressive censorship that caused people to fear for their lives or because of the harsh living conditions that compelled them to leave for purely economic reasons.

Évelyne Trouillot

Born in Port-au-Prince in 1954, Évelyne Trouillot spent her childhood and adolescence under the Duvalier dictatorship, growing up in a family of intellectuals who have contributed significantly to understanding, promoting, and enriching Haiti's vibrant cultural, educational, and historical landscape.[24] Trouillot's father taught history at the Petit Séminaire Collège Saint-Martial, a Catholic school founded in the nation's capital in 1872, and he later became a lawyer, serving as president of the bar in Haiti for several years. Working as a nurse in the medical center of a working-class neighborhood of Port-au-Prince, Trouillot's mother, Anne-Marie Morisset, would return home from work each day full of stories to tell Évelyne and her three siblings. As a young nurse she once crossed paths with François Duvalier, and she described to her children the dictator's evil, piercing gaze—although, as Évelyne notes, her mother's perception of Duvalier might very well have been influenced by her knowledge of the countless heinous acts he had committed.

The third of four children, Évelyne was not, like her older brother, sister, and cousins, an official member of the Rallye de l'effort, an association founded and supervised by priests from the Pères du Saint-Esprit congregation at the Petit Séminaire Collège Saint-Martial; she did, however, accompany them to various meetings and events. Although the group was not political per se, its emphasis on social issues did not sit well with the Duvalierist regime, which decreed it (like all other groups and gatherings) subversive. In a culmination of his ongoing conflict with the Roman Catholic Church, Duvalier ordered the expulsion of all Jesuit priests from Haiti in 1964—the same year Drouin and Numa, members of "The Thirteen," were publicly executed for their role in attempting to overthrow Duvalier.

Although Trouillot did not personally witness the assassination of Drouin and Numa, she, like generations of men and women in Haiti, was deeply marked by the Duvalier period. Noting how, growing up, "the world of writing was at once the most invited and the most honored [guest in our house]," she explained in an interview with Edwidge Danticat in 2005 to what extent her scholarly upbringing conflicted with the repressive atmosphere of the regime: "My most striking memory of the Duvalier dictatorship is still the image of the militiamen on the roof of the Chapelle Saint Antoine, a few meters from our home. And the imminent threat of searches in the houses in the quarter to find books deemed subversive. Then the feverish ha[s]te and the dull sound of books that one would get rid of in the latrines. This image of the condemned books remains for me one of the strongest images of the repression, this repression of knowledge and of creative freedom."[25]

Trouillot left Haiti with her mother and younger brother at age seventeen, in 1971, shortly after earning her high school diploma. Jean-Claude "Baby Doc" Duvalier had recently replaced his deceased father as president. While personal reasons contributed to her mother's departure from Haiti, the tense, oppressive atmosphere generated by the Duvalierist regime also factored significantly in her decision. Immigrating to the United States (New York and Florida), Trouillot attended college, studying languages and pedagogy. After Jean-Claude Duvalier fled Haiti in 1986, she returned the following year to Port-au-Prince, where she now lives, writes, and teaches French at the Université d'État d'Haïti. Trouillot has published works both in Creole and in French and is cofounder with her brother Lyonel and daughter, Nadève Ménard, of Pré-texte, a production company that organizes writing and reading workshops. After the 2010 earthquake, she created, with siblings Lyonel, Jocelyne, and Michel-Rolph, the Centre Culturel Anne-Marie Morisset as a way to provide children and young adults access to Haiti's wealth of cultural goods and artifacts; she also chronicled the devastating event in an op-ed piece published in the *New York Times*.[26]

Since the 1996 publication of her first collection of short stories, *La chambre interdite* (The forbidden room), Trouillot has published a broad array of literary texts that—through an impressive diversity of genres—address an extensive range of chapters from Haiti's complicated past. If a common theme traverses what over the past two decades has come to constitute her exceedingly rich oeuvre, it might best be described as the social and political maelstrom to which individuals have been subjected over the course of the country's history. Indeed, while Trouillot's works bear due testimony to the havoc wreaked on the country by natural disasters, the images with which she leaves her readers are seldom those of the hurricanes, flooding, and earthquakes that have—indelibly, it would seem—been etched for better or for worse on the world's consciousness. Rather, it is the impact and alarmingly inescapable nature of societal and human forces that are consistently articulated in Trouillot's works, and that, in compelling her characters to struggle as a means of individual and collective survival, render them in turn so compelling.

In relating the experiences of Lisette, a young house servant growing up on a plantation in the 1750s, *Rosalie l'infâme* (2003; *The Infamous Rosalie*, 2013)[27] paints a vivid portrait of slavery and slave revolt in the French colony of Saint-Domingue, providing an enlightening perspective on the loss and separation suffered due to colonization and the Middle Passage. Trouillot's illustrated children's book *L'île de Ti Jean* (Dapper, 2004; Little John's island) tells the magical tale of another young protagonist, Ti Jean, and his determination to bring about harmony in Haiti and—by extension—the world, employing an unassailable appreciation for and defense of the environment. Although set in the early 2000s, the meandering thoughts and memories of the aging narrator of the short story "Je m'appelle Fridhomme"[28] cast a harsh light on the American occupation of 1915–34, all the while contrasting the ever bitter taste that older generations have of that time period with the excitement that subsequent generations feel about the opportunity to live in the United States.

Depicting the myriad of personal and legal issues facing members of the Haitian diaspora, Trouillot has addressed issues related to immigration in other genres and settings as well. *Absences sans frontières* (Éditions Chèvre-feuille étoilée, 2013; Absences without borders) traces the long-distance relationship between Géraldine and her father, Gérard, whom, because he moved illegally to the United States in search of work before she was born, she has never met. In this work it is against the backdrop of Jean-Bertrand Aristide's short-lived presidency, General Raoul Cédras's bloody coup d'état, the US embargo on Haiti, September 11, and the Haitian earthquake of 2010 that relationships and identities alike are forged, sustained, and explored. And employing the dramatic device of a covered truck en route to an illegal border crossing to the Dominican Republic, Trouillot's award-winning play *Le bleu de l'île* (2012; *The Blue of the Island,* 2012)²⁹ frames the complex landscape of immigration in terms of the sacrifices that twelve Haitians are prepared to endure in choosing to leave their homeland.

Discussing *Le bleu de l'île* in 2010, Trouillot remarks, "I'm greatly drawn to the theme [of migration]. But there are other themes, such as the dictatorship—because we lived 30 years under the dictatorship of Duvalier *père* and *fils.* The effects of such hardship on the people, on love, on relationships between individuals in that environment, how those relationships evolved, the relations between the various social groups: those are the themes that Haitian writers address."³⁰ In the eponymous story of *La chambre interdite,* Trouillot broached the Duvalier dictatorship for the first time in her writings and, therein, the shroud of mystery that not only pervaded the period but in many ways exists to this day, haunting those who experienced it or who listened to the memories of those who did. Published in 2002, *Parlez-moi d'amour . . .* (Imprimerie Caraïbe, 2002; Speak to me of love) is a collection of short stories drawn from Trouillot's childhood: "They are true stories, even though I changed many of the circumstances; they are nightmares come true, facts that one would rather forget."³¹ One of the stories in the collection, "L'héritage des Chareron,"³² recounts how when members of the Chareron family are killed by the Tonton Macoutes, friends of the family neglect to pay their respects out of fear that they, too, will become targets of Duvalier's militia. *La mémoire aux abois* (Éditions Hoëbeke, 2010)—translated here as *Memory at Bay*—is Trouillot's first novel devoted fully to Duvalierism and the legacy it left to generations of Haitians.

The Duvalier Era in Haitian Literature

Censorship, brutality, and fear were commonplace during the three decades Duvalier *père* and *fils* remained in power; expressing dissent was extremely dangerous, punishable by death. Commenting on the status of literature under Duvalier, Yves Chemla notes in *Cultures Sud,* "For a long time, the violence that was carried out mollified fiction, with but only a few exceptions. The period defied words."[33] It is unsurprising, then, that the body of literature addressing the Duvalier period that was produced in Haiti from 1957 to 1971 is glaringly sparse. Those Haitians who did write or speak critically about the dictatorship were either killed (Jacques-Stephen Alexis) or forced into exile abroad (Gérard Étienne, Pierre Clitandre, Paul Laraque, Rassoul Labuchin).[34]

The most renowned literary work to date on the Duvalier era is one of the few texts written during the period itself—Marie Vieux-Chauvet's trilogy *Amour, colère, folie* (Paris: Gallimard, 1968; *Love, Anger, Madness: A Haitian Tragedy,* 2009).[35] Each of the three novellas offers a stark example of how Papa Doc's nightmarish reign affected those forced to live under its stifling restrictions and brazen corruption. Vieux-Chauvet originally believed she had succeeded in sufficiently disguising the harsh accusations leveled in her novel against the dictatorship. However, once the manuscript was accepted for publication by the prestigious French publishing house Gallimard, friends and acquaintances who read the text felt that her novel drew too-evident parallels to the Duvalier dictatorship and that, as a result, the novel would surely incur the regime's wrath. For example, as Laurent Dubois points out, "In 1962, the president had declared, 'I am even now an immaterial being,' and it was all too easy to conclude that Vieux-Chauvet's portrait of a ghostly, all-powerful leader was meant to describe him."[36] Madison Smartt Bell, noting that three members of the Vieux-Chauvet family had already been "lost" to the regime, explains, "Vieux-Chauvet persuaded Gallimard to withdraw [the book], while she went into permanent exile in New York City. . . . Her husband, Pierre Chauvet, made an emergency trip to Haiti, where he purchased as many copies of the book already in circulation there as he could recover—in order to destroy them."[37] The trilogy was eventually republished in 2005 (Paris: Maisonneuve & Larose/Emina Soleil) to great acclaim.

Although less well-known, Vieux-Chauvet's 1986 novel *Les rapaces* (Port-au-Prince: Imprimerie Henri Deschamps; The birds of prey),[38] levels in some ways a more unequivocally harsh portrait of the repressive Duvalier regime. Described as an autopsy of Haitian society of the 1970s and 1980s, the allegorical work (the three parts of which are entitled "The Cat," "The Poor," and "The Police"), set in Port-au-Prince, recounts the brutal reign of a tyrant son who in the book's opening pages ascends to power following an elaborate state funeral in honor of his deceased dictator father.[39]

In her 2010 interview with Danticat, Trouillot states with respect to the relative dearth of literary works on the Duvalier regime, "I think that we often tend not to face the pages of our history that upset us. I would have thought that there would be many more texts, many more stories around the Duvalier dictatorship."[40] Curiously, the vast majority of works on the period have been produced in the past twenty years.

Jan J. Dominique's *Mémoire d'une amnésique* (Port-au-Prince: Deschamps, 1984; *Memoir of an Amnesiac,* Coconut Creek, Florida: Caribbean Studies Press, 2008) illustrates the horror of living under the Duvalier regime, in particular as told by a woman (Paul) struggling to put into words the horrific events she endured at the time. The telling of Paul's story begins in 1957 upon her return from exile to Haiti, where, at the early age of six, she is forced to confront the social tensions of the country, the intrusion of the Tonton Macoutes on daily life, and, more generally, what is in effect another chapter of "a history of domination on Haitians."[41] After all, her father had—at the same age and while living in the very same house—experienced the invasion of American soldiers during the US occupation.[42]

Published a decade after *Mémoire d'une amnésique,* in 1994, Anne-christine d'Adesky's *Under the Bone* (New York: Farrar, Straus, and Giroux) further develops the systemic links between the two periods, "exhum[ing] the true terrors of the Duvalier regime as well as examin[ing] their military roots in the period during the 1915–1934 U.S. Occupation of Haiti."[43] Multiple storylines explore these connections, such as that of Gerard Metellus, a lawyer investigating the disappearance of missing persons, who—in concert with the United States—is also searching for the plunder the Duvaliers may have hidden away before fleeing the country, and that of Leslie Doyle, an American human rights activist who arrives in Haiti in 1986, soon after Jean-Claude Duvalier's departure, to research and compile the oral histories of women persecuted during the Duvalier era.

"La chambre bleue" ("The Blue Room") in Yanick Lahens's collection of short stories *Tante Resia et les dieux* (L'Harmattan, 1994; *Aunt Résia and the Spirits and Other Stories*, 2010),[44] is narrated by an adult who, in vividly recalling a particularly traumatic event in her childhood, is unable to come to grips with an experience that, years later, continues to haunt her. Although the reader is led to believe that some better understanding might be reached, the narrative, in returning to the "present" of the Duvalier era, is recounted through the eyes of a young child whose confused perspective is eerily emblematic of a period in Haiti's past that remains in many respects shrouded in uncertainty. "Les survivants" ("The Survivors") in the same collection focuses on the contagious nature of fear that a group of men feel—and share—in planning to undermine the regime.

In 1995, Edwidge Danticat published *Krik? Krak!* (Soho Press), a collection of short stories that examine the country's hardships from a variety of angles. "Children of the Sea" paints a particularly grim portrait by way of alternating narrators and lovers, one of whom has decided to flee the harsh environment of the Duvalier regime and set out by boat with thirty-six others in an attempt to forge a better life for himself. In Danticat's novel *The Dew Breaker* (Knopf, 2004), the violent past of a seemingly ordinary Haitian immigrant living in Brooklyn is gradually revealed. The man was in fact a member of the Tonton Macoutes in the 1960s, something he has hidden from those around him, including fellow immigrants whom he has himself tortured.

Marie-Célie Agnant's 2007 novel *Un alligator nommé Rosa* (Éditions du Remue-ménage; An alligator named Rosa) also deals with one of the members of Duvalier's dreaded arsenal—the torturer and executioner Rosa Bosquet (the maiden name of Madame Max Adolphe). Now into her seventies and ailing in southern France, Rosa is bedridden and desperately in need of someone able to care for her. At first glance, the mild-tempered, seemingly well-meaning Antoine Guibert appears to be the perfect fit. However, what is gradually divulged in Agnant's text is that Antoine's family was murdered at the hand of Rosa herself because of his journalist father's contentious writings. The sole survivor of the devastating house fire she set when he was ten, Antoine has waited forty years for the opportunity to exact his revenge.

Like *Un alligator nommé Rosa, Saisons sauvages* (Mercure, 2010; *Savage Seasons*, 2015),[45] by Kettly Mars, also emphasizes the dangers of being a journalist during the Duvalier period—especially when it comes to being editor-in-chief of a newspaper opposed to the regime, as is the case with Daniel Leroy. When Daniel's actions and increasingly overt critical stance lead to his abduction, his wife, Nirvah, pays a visit to the secretary of state for public safety, Raoul Vincent, to ask for information about her husband's whereabouts and to attempt to arrange his safe return. However, she soon realizes that in order to obtain favors from Raoul, she, in turn, will have to submit to his whims. As the novel progresses, it is increasingly less clear to what extent Nirvah continues to resist her new role as mistress, or if—quite to the contrary—the privileges that such a position afford her in fact outweigh the loss of her husband and reproachful eyes of her neighbors, friends, and relatives.

Memory at Bay: The Constraints of Intimacy

Personal correspondence with her agent in 2006 reveals that Évelyne Trouillot began work on *Memory at Bay* well before its publication in 2010,[46] contemplating early on the fictitious names of her characters, the human qualities of the dictator's widow, and where the plot should unfold. Despite appearing at first glance far removed in time and place from Haiti's Duvalier dictatorship, from its opening pages the completed novel can be read as a roman à clef: nearly all of the main characters (with the evident exception of Marie-Ange) represent a real-life person from the time period. Twenty-three-year-old Marie-Ange, a nurse's aide in a Parisian nursing home, has just been assigned to a new patient, Odile Savien Doréval, a decrepit woman in her eighties quickly nearing the end of her life. Of course, the hospice director's ironic comment, according to which any potential conflict of interest Marie-Ange might foresee with the patient is in fact irrelevant because, "in any case, this is no concern of yours" (5),[47] hints early on both at a key theme in the novel as well as at what is essentially the dilemma with which Marie-Ange will be faced: is it her duty to avenge her family and her country for the suffering and loss that can be traced directly back to the bedridden woman before her, or should her present professional responsibilities trump any such vendetta, personal or otherwise? In other words, because—as her boss is quick to point out—the dictator was already dead before Marie-Ange was born, does that preclude her right to effectively "get carried away" (5; or *exagérer*, in the original) by the burden of memories entrusted to her by her recently deceased mother? As the director's cautionary words suggest, it is alternately the assignment and appropriation of stories—willingly or otherwise—that constitute the crux of Trouillot's novel and that ultimately decide the fate of both protagonists.

Reflecting upon the impetus behind her writing, Trouillot has noted, "The social calls out to me. In Haiti, in fact, there are many things that call to creative people: injustices of all kinds, religious or sexual taboos, sadness, evil, lust for life. Personally I am fascinated by what constraint can create in people."[48] Perhaps in no other work by Trouillot are constraints—whether it be those capable of driving individuals or, conversely, those that stall them in their tracks—more palpable. For Marie-Ange, determining what barrier to erect between the past and present, between Haiti and France, is fundamental to her being able to grapple with her own identity and future. Her hope of moving forward with her life hinges on her ability to successfully identify and act upon these vexed juxtapositions, and yet when, like her mother before her, she starts responding to the countless e-mails and phone calls arriving from Haiti, the difficulty of negotiating such juxtapositions confuses the clarity with which she desires to act: "I tried to resist the abyss of knotty problems, the morass of difficulties with their thorny tangles. But what drew me inexorably were the silences, the ellipses and dead spaces, the voids infiltrated by a mute perplexity. The moments of drift in which despair overpowers all of life and stifles all expression. . . . These contacts [with troubled young Quisque-yans] throw me into a world where reality nudges me along and shakes up my memory" (101).

In contrast to her caretaker, the vast majority of events that Odile Savien Doréval evokes from her past are recalled with satisfaction and, moreover, in a state of quiet reserve: "Silence is ultimately the surest means of control. . . . The only solution lay in her ability to curtail all communication with the outside world" (5). Odile's memories take the form of calculated moral and philosophical justifications, not only with respect to her own imperious ethos but in terms of the draconian measures employed by her husband and son. In short, "governing a nation entails sacrifice. As their great friend Lambert Chambral used to say, 'A good Dorévalist is always ready to murder his children, the children to eliminate their parents'" (27). Whereas Marie-Ange often resents the memories with which she is burdened—"I detest this dour gravity I inherited from you" (104)—Odile dreads the growing frequency with which her memory has begun to fail her: "She realized that it was becoming more and more of a strain for her to think about all that, but she focused single-mindedly on her snatches of memory" (75).

Trouillot's descriptions of the declining state of Odile's mental acuity, her modest origins, the apparent innocence of her early ambitions, and her desire to be eventually "if not loved, then at least understood" (103) by her caretaker offer an intimate and even sympathetic view of the wife of Haiti's most notoriously corrupt and deadly leader. By presenting an unexpectedly human side of Simone Ovide Duvalier, Trouillot challenges readers in much the same way that Marie-Ange herself is challenged. Marie-Ange must confront the disquieting image of her (family's and country's) past as an inseparable part of her own existence, as readers in turn struggle to reconcile the portrait of a generally reviled person who nonetheless has genuinely human (and even humane) characteristics not unlike those of Marie-Ange herself—including those of feeling fear, loneliness, and a fundamental desire to be understood. In this respect, the constraints that Trouillot's text impose upon the reader introduce a sense of startling intimacy with those responsible for the horrors, despite the unquestionable damage that the Duvalier regime (*père* and *fils*) inflicted on Haiti in terms of human lives, financial resources, and sustainable development.

It is important to note that by juxtaposing the narratives of Odile and Simone in *Memory at Bay,* Trouillot provides a perspective that is by definition not one-sided. The narrative by which we come to know the dictator's widow, while humanizing her to the extent that we sense her insecurities, emotions, and even warmth, also casts shadows on her, placing her just out of reach of our full comprehension. As if subject to the same progressing senility as Odile, we as readers are increasingly forced to question our view of her and, consequently, to question how and why we might ultimately condemn or forgive her. After all, any potential position we might take is based on perceptions that prove to be just as unfounded and subjective as they are defensible.

Although Simone Duvalier was never a political figure on a national scale, some historians have contended that she played an instrumental role behind the scenes.[49] In Trouillot's novel, it is fittingly difficult to detect where Odile's decisions and actions overlap with those of her husband, Fabien: "She knew how to take revenge without fretting over it, striking hard and accurately" (112). Similarly, the subtle, clever manner with which Odile attempts to conceal the true state of her lucidity from Marie-Ange can be read as suggestive of the woman who, following her husband's death, ensured the continuation of the family dynasty by personally making decisions for her nineteen-year-old son at the start of his presidency:[50] "Her chest subsided farther under the weight of an inaudible sigh. Feeling more than seeing the circumspect gaze of the young aide turn toward her, she quickly recast her features to those of a decrepit old lady with lifeless eyes" (73).

Marie-Ange's native land may seem somewhat enigmatic to readers, but Quisqueya is one of the names given by indigenous populations, before the arrival of Christopher Columbus, to Hispaniola—the island shared today by Haiti and the Dominican Republic. In addition, semantic and phonetic similarities make it possible to match the deceased Fabien Doréval to dictator François Duvalier, Odile Savien Doréval to Simone Ovide Duvalier, the Fort Décembre prison to that of Fort Dimanche, Port-du-Roi to Port-au-Prince, Rallye de l'effort to Rally for Friendship, and more. By way of these key markers, it is further possible to link other references in the novel to important events and figures in Haitian history, such as the assassination of Numa and Drouin, the extravagant wedding of Jean-Claude Duvalier to Michèle Bennett in May 1980, Simone and François Duvalier's appreciation of Vodou, and the death of François Duvalier.

Trouillot's borderline ludic substitution of fictitious names for those of actual people in *Memory at Bay* is clearly not akin to Vieux-Chauvet's desire and (unsuccessful) attempt to disguise *Love, Anger, Madness*'s indictment of François Duvalier. Avoiding real names provides Trouillot with a greater liberty to mix fiction and reality; after all, as a work of literature, the work is not meant to be a precise historical account of the Duvalier regime. Moreover, not identifying specific names, dates, and events opens the text to a potentially broader range of interpretations; the silent, painful struggle that ensues between Marie-Ange and Odile is not unique to the legacy of Duvalierism or Haiti, and it poignantly depicts the at times both fragile and brutal nature of social and political relationships irrespective of time or place. Clearly, Trouillot's intention was not to write a subversive narrative whose "code" would remain deeply embedded within the text but instead to allow for reflection on the tenuous relationship between the past and the present, the personal and the public, as well as the real and the imagined of all historical events.

In this regard, Marie-Ange and Odile's alternating narratives reflect the inherently dynamic nature of social struggle in proving to be both correspondent and contradictory. In one respect, the memories recounted by each protagonist match: places, people, and predicaments, as well as preoccupations relative to family and country, echo one another. With frequently overlapping place markers, events, and emotions, the two narratives can be understood to correspond, albeit in a strained, eerily silent manner. However, without fail, the parallel versions of the past recounted by Marie-Ange and Odile prove incongruous—because the memories they have are, respectively, either those of individuals who suffered grave injustices at the hands of the regime or of those responsible for causing these very same injustices. The inexorable constraints of memory in the novel are born of this profound tension. Short of taking action, of doing away with the image judged to be unfaithful or incompatible, how does one resolve the pain of ever-divergent memories? What role should our memories, and those of others, play in our ability to determine right from wrong, action from inaction? For Marie-Ange and Odile, the unsettled notions of impunity and forgiveness are, agonizingly, further blurred by forgetfulness. Whether desired but impossible, or shunned but unavoidable, forgetting is, like memory, an individual phenomenon with profoundly social implications. Coincidentally, Jean-Claude "Baby Doc" Duvalier's unexpected return to Haiti one year after the publication of *Memory at Bay* has forced generations of Haitians to grapple with the constraints of a suddenly intimate past. Indeed, an important chapter of Haiti's collective history depends in part on how the Duvalier era is remembered today.[51]

Notes

1. "Jean-Claude 'Baby Doc' Duvalier returns to Haiti," *Telegraph*, www .telegraph.co.uk/news/worldnews/8264366/Jean-Claude-Baby-Doc-Duva lier-returns-to-Haiti.html?image=3.

2. Belmondo Ndengue, "Jean-Claude Duvalier: L'incroyable retour," *Le Nouvelliste*, January 18, 2011, http://lenouvelliste.com/lenouvelliste/article print/87884.html.

Michèle Montas, the journalist and widow of the journalist Jean-Léopold Dominique, who was assassinated in 2002, was the first public figure to openly disapprove of Duvalier's return and appearance on the Haitian political scene.

3. The report questioned the validity of the first round of the 2010–11 Haitian presidential election held on November 28, and it effectively prevented President Préval's own Unity (INITE) Party candidate, Jude Célestin, from participating in the second round, to be held only three weeks after Duvalier's return to Haiti.

4. Ndengue, "Jean-Claude Duvalier: L'incroyable retour."

5. Ginger Thompson, "In Haiti, Return of Duvalier Reopens Old Wounds," *New York Times*, January 29, 2011, www.nytimes.com/2011/01/30/world/americas/30haiti.html?pagewanted=all&_r=0.

6. Lemoine Bonneau, "À qui profite l'arrivée de Jean-Claude Duvalier?" *Le Nouvelliste*, January 17, 2011, http://lenouvelliste.com/lenouvelliste/articleprint/87924.html.

7. While the number of individuals who have filed human rights complaints against Duvalier has climbed to thirty as of April 2014, this represents a small fraction of the number of people who were either tortured or know of others who were killed or simply disappeared during Baby Doc's fifteen-year reign.

8. "Haiti renews passport for ex-dictator Duvalier," *USA Today*, January 5, 2013. http://www.usatoday.com/story/news/world/2013/01/05/haiti-duvalier-passport/1811483/

9. As the first democratically elected president of Haiti, Aristide served two incomplete terms (1991, 1994–1996; 2001–2004). In 2004, Aristide left Haiti under disputed circumstances and eventually took up residence in South Africa, where he lived in exile for seven years before returning to Haiti in 2011.

10. A well-placed member of François Duvalier's Presidential Guard and close financial adviser to Jean-Claude Duvalier, "the intelligent Prosper Avril" briefly became president of Haiti (1988–1990) after leading a military coup against the transition government of Leslie Manigat that was set in place after Duvalier *fils* fled the country in 1986.

11. Danio Darius, "Jean-Claude Duvalier aux Gonaïves, la présidence s'explique sur l'invitation," *Le Nouvelliste*, January 9, 2014, http://lenouvelliste.com/lenouvelliste/articleprint/126055.html.

12. Jean-Robert Fleury, "Les minutes de l'audition de Jean-Claude Duvalier," *Le Nouvelliste*, March 1, 2013, http://lenouvelliste.com/lenouvelliste/articleprint/114014.html.

13. William Booth, "In Haiti, Former Dictator 'Baby Doc' Duvalier Is Thriving," *Washington Post*, January 17, 2012, http://www.washington

post.com/world/americas/in-haiti-the-former-dictator-duvalier-thrives/2012
/01/13/gIQAaYbM6P_story.html.

14. In February 2014, a three-judge panel ruled that Duvalier should indeed stand trial for allegations he tortured, killed, and imprisoned opponents.

15. Danièle Magloire, "Nous n'oublierons pas ce qu'a été la dictature duvaliériste!" *Le Nouvelliste*, April 24, 2013, http://lenouvelliste.com/lenou velliste/articleprint/116058.html

16. Thompson, "In Haiti, Return of Duvalier Reopens Old Wounds."

17. Richard A. Haggerty, ed., *Haiti: A Country Study* (Washington: GPO for the Library of Congress, 1989), http://countrystudies.us/haiti/17.htm.

18. "The Death and Legacy of Papa Doc Duvalier," *Time*, January 17, 2011, http://content.time.com/time/magazine/article/0,9171,876967,00.html.

19. "L'état duvaliérien," *Haïti lutte contre l'impunité*, www.haitilutte contre-impunite.org/index_by_tag/2?locale=fr.

20. Etzer Charles, *Le pouvoir politique en Haïti de 1957 à nos jours* (Éditions Karthala, 1994), 265, my translation.

21. Known also as Rosalie Bosquet (her maiden name) during the time she served under François Duvalier as prison warden of Fort Dimanche, Madame Max Adolphe also came to serve as commander in chief of the Tonton Macoutes, a position she held for more than twenty years, until Jean-Claude Duvalier fled Haiti in 1986.

22. Edwidge Danticat, *Create Dangerously: The Immigrant Artist at Work* (New York: First Vintage Books, 2011).

23. Laurent Dubois, *Haiti: The Aftershocks of History* (New York: Picador, 2012), 354.

24. Évelyne's uncle, Henock Trouillot, was a historian, novelist, and playwright; her younger brother, Lyonel, is, like Évelyne, an award-winning writer, perhaps most noted for his novels *Yanvalou pour Charlie* (Arles: Actes Sud, 2009, Prix Wepler-Fondation la Poste; The wake for Charlie) and *Parabole du failli* (Arles: Actes Sud, 2013, Prix Carbet de la Caraïbe et du Tout-Monde; The parable of failure); Jocelyne, Évelyne's sister, is a leading educational expert and chancellor at the Université Caraïbes in Haiti, as well as an author of pedagogical texts and children's books in Creole; Évelyne's older brother, Michel-Rolph, was a renowned professor of anthropology and of social sciences at the University of Chicago who authored seminal theoretical works on Haitian culture and politics, such as *Haiti: State against Nation: The Origins and Legacies of Duvalierism* (New York: Monthly Review Press, 1990) and *Silencing the Past: Power and the Production of History* (Boston: Beacon Press, 1995). Michel-Rolph's death in 2012 elicited homages from around the world, including an academic symposium at New York University in March 2013 and a special issue devoted to him and his works in the *Journal of Haitian Studies* 19.2 (Fall 2013).

25. "Évelyne Trouillot," interview by Edwidge Danticat, *Bomb* 90 (Winter 2005), http://bombmagazine.org/article/2708/evelyne-trouillot.

26. Évelyne Trouillot, "Aftershocks," *New York Times,* January 20, 2010, http://www.nytimes.com/2010/01/21/opinion/21trouillot.html?_r=0.

27. *Rosalie l'infâme* received the Prix de la romancière francophone du Club Soroptimist de Grenoble (2004) and was published in English as *The Infamous Rosalie,* trans. Marjorie Attignol Salvodon (Lincoln: University of Nebraska Press, 2013).

28. Évelyne Trouillot, "My Name Is Fridhomme," trans. Jason Herbeck, *Caribbean Writer* 25 (2011): 206–12.

29. Although not published until 2012, *Le bleu de l'île* was performed much earlier and received the Beaumarchais award from l'Écriture Théâtrale de la Caraïbe in 2005.

30. Anne-Claire Veluire, "Haïti: La littérature pour exorciser la catastrophe," *Cultures sans frontières,* March 28, 2010, http://www.radio.cz/fr/article/126393 (my translation).

31. "Évelyne Trouillot," interview by Edwidge Danticat.

32. The story was published in English as "The Chareron Inheritance," trans. Avriel Goldberger, in *Words without Borders: The World through the Eyes of Writers—An Anthology,* (New York: Anchor Books, 2007), 311–22.

33. Yves Chemla, "Kettly Mars, *Saisons sauvages,*" *Cultures Sud,* my translation, www.culturessud.com/contenu.php?id=157.

34. Although the death of Alexis has never been confirmed, it is believed that he and four friends were arrested, tortured, and executed by the Tonton Macoutes in 1961.

After going into exile in Canada in 1964, the poet and novelist Étienne wrote, for instance, *Le nègre crucifié* (Éditions Francophone et Nouvelle Optique, 1974; *Crucified in Haiti,* trans. Claudia Harris, Montréal: Éditions du Marais, 2006) and *Un ambassadeur macoute à Montréal* (Nouvelle Optique, 1979; A Macoute ambassador in Montreal).

In 1980, Clitandre, along with other journalists such as the renowned Radio Inter broadcaster Jean Dominique, was expelled from Haiti. His novel *Cathédrale du mois d'août* (Port-au-Prince: Fardin, 1979; *Cathedral of the August Heat,* trans. Bridget Jones, New York: Readers International, 1987) chronicles the extreme poverty and brutal militiamen of Port-au-Prince under Duvalier.

As a poet who counts among the first generation of Haitians to write in Creole, Laraque went into exile (United States and Spain) in 1961 after being dismissed from the military. His works include *Les armes quotidiennes—Poésie quotidienne* (La Havane: Casa de las Americas, 1979; Daily weapons—Daily poetry) and *Le vieux nègre et l'exil* (Paris: Silex, 1988; The old negro and exile). His poem "Exile Is Stale Bread" was published in *Open Gate: An Anthology of Haitian Creole Poetry,* eds. Paul Laraque and Jack Hirschman (Chicago: Northwestern University Press, 2001), 25.

The poet, actor, playwright, and founder of the Mouvement Théâtral Ouvrier, Labuchin was captured and imprisoned in Fort Dimanche three times before being sent into exile in France in 1982 for the remainder of Baby Doc's rule. His poem "Tonton Macoutes Steal Dreams" can be found in *Open Gate*, 29.

For a detailed discussion of writing and terror during the Duvalier era, see Joseph F. Ferdinand, "Doctrines littéraires et climats politiques sous les Duvalier," in *Écrire en pays assiégé—Haiti—Writing under Siege*, eds. Marie-Agnès Sourieau and Kathleen M. Balutansky (New York: Rodopi, 2004), 193–230.

35. Marie Vieux-Chauvet, *Love, Anger, Madness: A Haitian Tragedy*, trans. Rose-Miriam Réjouis and Val Vinokur (New York: Modern Library, 2009).

36. Laurent Dubois, *Haiti: The Aftershocks of History* (New York: Picador, 2012), 313.

37. Madison Smartt Bell, "Permanent Exile: On Marie Vieux-Chauvet," *Nation*, February 1, 2010, www.thenation.com/article/permanent-exile-ma rie-vieux-chauvet.

38. *Les rapaces* was published posthumously under the author's maiden name, Marie Vieux. Vieux, divorced from her husband, died in Brooklyn, New York, in 1973.

39. See Dieulermession Petit-Frère, "Relire 'Les rapaces' de Marie Vieux Chauvet," *Le Nouvelliste*, October 4, 2012, http://lenouvelliste.com/lenou velliste/article/109523/Relire-Les-Rapaces-de-Marie-Vieux-Chauvet.html.

40. "Évelyne Trouillot," interview by Edwidge Danticat.

41. Myriam J. A. Chancy, *Framing Silence: Revolutionary Novels by Haitian Women* (New Brunswick, New Jersey: Rutgers University Press, 1997), 92.

42. Another notable exception when it comes to literary works addressing the Duvalier era published prior to the 1990s is *Mémoire en colinmaillard* (Montréal: Éditions Nouvelle Optique, 1976; Memory in blind man's buff) by Anthony Phelps, which recounts events taking place over the course of the morning and early afternoon of September 23 (most likely, 1969), viewed from the vantage point of the protagonist's balcony.

43. Chancy, 143.

44. Yanick Lahens, *Aunt Résia and the Spirits and Other Stories*, trans. Betty Wilson (Charlottesville: University of Virginia Press, 2010).

45. Kettly Mars, *Savage Seasons*, trans. Jeanine Herman (Lincoln: University of Nebraska Press, 2015).

46. The novel was awarded the Prix Carbet de la Caraïbe et du Tout-Monde (2010).

47. In the original French, the expression used by Trouillot—"ce ne sont pas vos histoires" (7)—is particularly telling as, literally, it means "these stories are not yours."

48. "Évelyne Trouillot," interview by Edwidge Danticat.

49. Alix Michel, *Manières haïtiennes: Le combat pour implanter démocratie et capitalisme dans la première république nègre* (Xlibris, 2013), 124. Michel reports in his study that he was unable to find any trace of speeches or political appearances organized by Simone Duvalier. See also Laurent Dubois, *Haiti: The Aftershocks of History* (New York: Picador, 2012), 321.

50. Alix Michel, *Manières haïtiennes*, 125.

51. Jean-Claude Duvalier died of a heart attack on October 4, 2014, at the age of sixty-three. Following an initial tweet by Haitian president Michel Martelly, who referred to the former dictator as "an authentic son of Haiti," and the declaration of Martelly's spokesman suggesting that, according to proper protocol, a state funeral would be warranted, public outrage in Haiti and the international community soon convinced the administration to deny Duvalier an official ceremony. He was buried on October 11 after a family ceremony at a chapel in Port-au-Prince.

CPSIA information can be obtained
at www.ICGtesting.com
Printed in the USA
LVHW040011080723
751729LV00003B/423